LOVE IN TUSCANY

TRUE LOVE TRAVELS BOOK THREE

POPPY PENNINGTON-SMITH

Love in the Rockies

Love in Provence

Love in Tuscany

Love in The Highlands

Love at Christmas

Love in the Alps – Subscriber Exclusive

First published 2020 by Bewick Press Ltd.

BEWICK PRESS LTD, MAY 2020
Copyright © 2020 Poppy Pennington-Smith.

www.bewickpress.com
www.poppypennington.com

CHAPTER 1

The last time Rose was on a plane, she was eleven years old. It had not been a pleasant experience. The turbulence on board had been so dreadful that she'd ended up vomiting into a paper bag for most of the journey. And this horror had been compounded by the fact that, on what was supposed to be a family holiday to Tenerife, her parents had decided to get divorced.

Now, twenty years later, Rose was sitting beside her best friend Katie, having her ankles bashed by the passing hostess trolley, and trying not to think about the fact she was thousands of feet in the air.

"I didn't know you hated flying." Katie was casually flicking through a celebrity gossip magazine and sipping on a lukewarm coffee.

"I don't hate it." Rose shuffled in her seat. "I just don't *like* it."

Katie stopped flicking and looked at her. "Rose, don't take this the wrong way but this was supposed to be a chance for you to relax." Katie emphasised the word *relax* as if Rose didn't know what it meant.

She sighed and closed her eyes, willing the tension that had gripped her shoulders to dissolve. "I know. I'm sorry."

"Don't say sorry, just..." Katie handed her the magazine. "Here. Just try to distract yourself, yeah? We'll be there soon."

Rose nodded and smiled, making an effort to look as if she was feeling better already – just from holding on to the glossy pages in front of her. But she wasn't feeling better. As always, anxiety was bubbling just below the surface of her skin for no particular reason that she could fathom.

As she thought about where they were heading, the bubbling gave way to prickling.

Soon, they'd be landing in Rome and climbing into a cab. That cab would drive them through the rolling Tuscany landscape for about two hours until, eventually, they'd reach a sprawling ranch owned by Katie's older brother Thomas.

Part-ranch and part-retreat, Katie had persuaded Rose to accompany her on her annual visit to Heart of the Hills. But Rose was *not* looking forward to it.

She'd agreed because Katie had pestered and pestered and pestered about it for weeks but, deep down, she was wishing she'd stuck to her usual holiday spot on the Norfolk coast – far away from people and *horses*.

Rose's dislike of flying was nothing compared to her feelings about horses. She wasn't just 'not a fan' of them; she was *terrified* of them. Katie had assured her that she could just sunbathe in the gardens, swim in the pool, and avoid all contact with them. But the mere thought of being in close proximity with goodness-knows-how-many horses was starting to make her feel woozy.

Rose breathed in and gripped the scratchy, plastic arms of her seat.

"Ladies and gentleman, please return your seats to the upright position. We will soon begin our descent into Rome."

THREE HOURS LATER

Rose stumbled out of the taxi feeling sick to her stomach. Their driver had travelled at such a break-neck speed that even Katie had needed to stick her head out of the window to prevent nausea from kicking in.

Rose was breathing slowly and deliberately, counting to ten, when her best friend squealed and rushed forwards.

"Tommy!!"

"All right, Little Sis', how you doing?"

Rose looked up and saw Katie wrapping her arms around someone she barely recognised as being Thomas Goodwin, Katie's older brother.

The Thomas Goodwin that Rose remembered had been podgy, pale, and battling teenage acne. But *this* Thomas was the opposite; he was broad-shouldered, tanned, and wearing a neatly shaped beard and a pair of red cowboy boots that made him look like something straight out of an old Western movie.

As he stepped around his sister and extended his hand to take Rose's, she swallowed hard and tried to find her voice.

"Thomas..." was all she could manage.

Thomas tilted his head sideways and flashed her an almost too-white smile. "Hey there, Rose. How are you? It's been years." He stepped back and rested his hands on his hips. "You look good."

Rose began to blush. She was wearing jeans, scruffy sandals and a plain grey T-shirt. Her hair was scraped back into a messy ponytail and her makeup felt like it had faded to the point of non-existence; she did *not* look good.

"Tom," Katie warned. "Rose is off limits. Okay?" She looked at her brother and laughed, which made Rose blush even harder.

"Hey, I'm just being friendly." Thomas ruffled Katie's hair, then looked back at Rose and shrugged innocently. "She seems to think I'm–"

"A cad?" Katie teased.

"Well, actually that's quite a nice way of putting it. Thank you."

Rose tried to shake herself loose from her stunned silence and laughed nervously. "A *cad?*"

Thomas was already turning away and beckoning for them to follow him towards the main ranch house, but Katie leaned in and said, "Someone who like the ladies. A lot."

"Oh." Rose hadn't ever pictured Thomas Goodwin as someone who'd have the chance to like women too much, even if he wanted to. But, clearly, he'd changed.

"He has a different girlfriend every week," Katie laughed. "So, just watch out."

Rose looked down at her clothes and tugged at the hem of her T-shirt. "I don't think you've got anything to worry about, Katie."

Katie stopped abruptly and turned, putting her hands on Rose's arms. "Now. Listen. I want you to stop all this self-deprecating nonsense. You're a gorgeous, strong, independent woman." She glanced over at Thomas. "Tommy always liked you. And I can tell by the way he's looking at you that, given half a chance, he'll try it on. But trust me – you need a *decent* guy, Rose. And my brother, as much as I love him, is *not* that guy." Katie started walking again and looped her arm through Rose's. "Besides, best friends and brothers don't date. It's a disaster waiting to happen."

CHAPTER 2

The main ranch house was a sprawling wooden building with a wrap-around terrace, a swing that reminded Rose of the kind she always swooned after in wholesome American movies, and large double doors that welcomed them inside.

The floor of the entrance hall was made of flagstones and, looking around at the crisp white walls, she instantly felt cooler.

Beside her, Thomas reached behind the vacant reception desk, grabbed a key and handed it to Katie. "Gave you one of the best cabins."

Katie grinned. "Same as last time?"

"Yep."

Bouncing up and down on the balls of her feet, Katie turned to Rose and said, "Just *wait* until you see the view."

Hoping they would head there straight away, so she

could have a lie down and recalibrate, Rose glanced back at the doors.

"You guys hungry?" Thomas was leaning against the desk. He was wearing a crisp white T-shirt and jeans, and Rose couldn't stop looking at his ridiculous red cowboy boots; she felt as if she should laugh at them, but somehow they suited him. They were almost the exact same shade as the pair of sandals she'd packed at the last minute and which now lay somewhere in the depths of her suitcase.

His hair was darker and fuller than she remembered, and somehow his beard had changed the entire shape of his face. Usually, she hated beards. But this one made his jaw look strong and square and...

"Rose?" Katie nudged her and she instantly began to blush.

"Sorry," Rose said quickly, looking away from Thomas and down at her feet. Her toenails were bare. She really should have painted them before leaving home.

"Are you all right?" Katie ducked to catch her eyes.

"Sorry," Rose repeated, still trying not to look at Thomas because, for some reason, his presence was making her feel all kinds of flustered. "Still a bit woozy from the journey. Perhaps I should go lie down for a bit."

Katie was nodding at her sympathetically when Thomas interrupted. "Nonsense, best cure for travel sickness is to get some food in your belly."

Rose couldn't think of anything worse than eating, but

she smiled a thin smile and found herself saying, "Sure, okay. Food would be good."

"Great. You two head on out back and I'll tell the kitchen to rustle something up." Thomas thumped Rose gently on the shoulder, then did the same to his sister. "You know the way."

"Sure do." Katie took Rose's hand and took her back out of the double doors they had come through, past the porch swing, and all the way around to the rear of the building.

"Wow," Rose said, stopping as they rounded the corner. "What a view."

"I know, right? Thomas is a pain in the neck but he's done a pretty good job with this place."

"It's incredible." Rose stepped forward, taking in the wooden deck that looked out at the rest of the ranch. In front of her, the sensational Tuscan landscape stretched as far as she could see and she had no idea how much of it belonged to Thomas. She couldn't even remember how he'd ended up owning the ranch. When they'd known each other as kids, he'd been all set to go off to university and study... what was it? Maths? Business?

To the left, a neat but rough around the edges dirt track led past clusters of trees and curved out of sight. Directly in front of them, a rich green lawn gave way to a large sparkling swimming pool. Beyond the pool, rolling hills and cypress trees told her she was most definitely in the central region of Italy. And to the right, the cabins that were – according to the website – the 'jewel in the crown' of *Heart of the Hills* stood proudly beside one another.

Rose heard herself sigh contentedly and realised that she was feeling a little better.

Beside her, Katie had flopped down at a table and taken her sunglasses off. Above them, a vine covered trellis provided a canopy of lightly dappled shade and Rose sat down too, leaning back in her chair and trying to remember if she'd ever been anywhere as beautiful as Thomas' ranch.

"You know," Katie sighed. "I really should do something nice for Tommy someday to say thank you for letting me come here every year." She paused and laughed. "But then, maybe free holidays for life is payment for all the times he beat me up when we were kids."

"I'm very glad I don't have a brother," Rose said solemnly; she liked her solitary existence as an only child.

"Oh, I don't know. It might have been good for you." Katie nudged her chair closer and pulled Rose in to pose for a selfie. "Loosen you up a bit."

"I'm perfectly loose, thank you."

Katie sat back and pouted. "Oh, are you now?"

Again, Rose began to blush. "You know what I mean."

Katie opened her mouth to reply, but then her eyes widened and she said, "Ooh. Food."

Behind them, a large middle-aged woman, with possibly the most jovial expression Rose had ever seen, emerged from inside holding a tray of meats, cheeses, olives, figs and roasted peppers.

She set it down on the table in front of Rose and Katie, and grinned at them. "All our own produce," she said in a heavy, lilting Italian accent. "Best prosciutto in Tuscany." She waved her hand and continued to stand behind them, smiling. "Try, try…"

Almost instantly, Katie reached out and plucked an olive and a piece of prosciutto from the platter. "Wonderful!" she said, smacking her lips and grinning.

Rose did the same and nodded in agreement. "Very good," she said. Then she sat up a little straighter in her chair and looked back towards the ranch doors. "Is Thomas joining us?"

The chef shook her head. "Mister Goodwin had some errands. He asked me to tell you that he will see you later."

Katie shrugged and rolled her eyes. "Typical of my big brother. Always so busy. He'll work himself into the ground one of these days."

The cook nodded sincerely. "Mister Goodwin works very, very hard." Then she waved at them and headed inside.

Rose thanked her and turned back to their lunch, trying to ignore the little twist of disappointment she'd felt when Thomas had not reappeared.

"The food here is incredible. They have a small-holding and grow all their own fruit and veg. It's like paradise, to be honest." Katie was tucking into the olives and talking with her mouth half full. "Sometimes, I think I should just give up on the practice and move out here to be a horse-hand."

"Would you really?" The thought of Katie leaving England instantly made Rose feel nauseous.

Katie looked at her and laughed. "No, not really. It's a nice dream though."

"I thought you loved your work?"

"I do. Of course I do." She bit her lower lip, suddenly seeming more serious. "It does get a bit much sometimes though – counselling other people through their problems. Doesn't leave much room for problems of your own."

"But you know I'm always here to counsel you," Rose said, smiling at her friend.

"Of course I do."

"I'd hate it if you left."

"And that's the other reason why I never would," Katie grinned. Then she gestured to the roasted peppers. "Try these... amazing."

Rose sighed. This was what she loved about Katie; despite the fact that she spent her days helping people with very serious problems, she always managed to stay light and happy – a little ray of sunshine. Rose leaned in to rest her head on Katie's shoulder. Katie balanced her chin on the top of Rose's head and put her arm around her shoulders.

"I love you, Rosie."

"I love you too, Katie."

"You promise we'll be best friends forever?"

"I promise."

This was a routine they'd had since they were teenagers; Katie always asked her if they'd be friends forever and Rose *always* replied 'I promise'.

They were barely even thirteen when they first met but they had become instant best friends for life. Nothing had ever come between them. And nothing ever would.

CHAPTER 3

*A*fter finishing their homegrown Italian lunch, Katie took Rose down to the cabin Thomas had reserved for them. It was small but spacious and had an incredible view over the ranch, with big picture windows, a patio enclosed by a low flint wall, and a fire pit they could light when it got dark.

Rose immediately began to unpack, folding her things and putting them neatly into drawers, but Katie sat on the edge of the bed, watching her quizzically.

"Fancy a swim?" She grinned, jiggling her feet impatiently.

"Swim?" Rose glanced at her half-empty case. She'd hoped to avoid getting into her bathing costume for a little longer. Usually, she chose vacations where swimwear was not required. Hiking through wet and dreary English countryside or reading curled up beside a roaring fire was more Rose's style.

"Yes. Swim." Katie looked towards the patio doors. "It's so lovely out there, Rose. Come on."

And before Rose could object, Katie was grabbing a bikini from the top of her case and dashing into the bathroom to change.

Alone in the bedroom, Rose examined the options she'd brought with her. All one-pieces, she had the same design in black, red, and green.

She chose black, removed her travel clothes and quickly shimmied into it, then grabbed her towel and her book.

Out by the pool, they were the only ones there.

"It's usually pretty quiet," Katie said, heading straight for the water. "Most people ride all day and swim before dinner."

"Are you going to ride while we're here?" Rose set her things down gently on a nearby lounger and tip-toed towards the edge of the pool.

"Probably." Katie was already in and looked up at her. "But only if you don't mind."

"Of course not." Rose sat down on the edge and dipped her toes into the cool water. "I told you - just because I'm not a fan of horses, doesn't mean you have to avoid them."

Katie smiled. Her eyes twinkled. And before Rose's brain could relay the interpretation that her friend was about to do something mischievous, Katie had grabbed Rose by the ankles and tugged her straight in to the water.

Rose emerged spluttering, with water in her eyes and a grin on her face. "I knew you were going to do that."

"And yet you didn't stop me," Katie said.

"I'll get you back."

"You'll have to catch me first!" Katie yelled as she swam off towards the other end of the pool.

Rose raced after her, but after their initial burst of energy subsided, they spent the rest of the afternoon alternating between sunbathing and cooling down in the water.

By the time early-evening approached, Rose was pretty sure she'd caught the sun on her cheeks and Katie announced that she was starving.

"Shall we head back?"

"Sure." Rose was towel-drying her hair and getting ready to gather her things when she heard a voice in the distance shout, "You two had a good day?"

Looking up, she saw Thomas. He was still wearing his red cowboy boots and was waving as he approached. Quickly, Rose wrapped herself in her towel and gave her hair a shake.

Beside her, Katie had shrugged a floaty kaftan over her head and slipped her feet back into her sandals. "An amazing day. Five stars from us so far, big bro."

"The pool is wonderful," Rose added, still unfathomably tongue tied in Thomas' presence.

Slowly, Thomas sat down on a nearby lounger, resting

his elbows on his knees and leaning forwards. "Built it with my own hands," he said, nodding at the swimming pool.

"Yeah, yeah. You're so big and strong, Tommy." Katie rolled her eyes.

Thomas grinned at her, then looked at Rose and pretended to flex his muscles.

Rose blinked, looked away, and willed herself not to blush. "You really built it?" She glanced at the pool. She was holding onto her towel, gripping it tightly in case a sudden gust of wind whipped it out of her hands.

"Sure did."

"Rose, please," Katie interrupted. "Don't get him started - we'll be here for hours if he lists all the *ingenious* things he's done since he took over."

Katie was joking – making fun of her brother the way she always did – but, despite the fact it was nothing more than banter, Rose noticed Thomas' grin falter.

"I'd like to hear about it," she said. "Do you have pictures of what it used to be like?"

"Right!" Katie grabbed Rose's arm, laughing. "That's enough. The ranch is wonderful and Tommy is very, very clever but he can tell you about it later. Right now, we need clothes and food, in that order."

Rose allowed Katie to start dragging her back towards the cabin. She expected Thomas to follow them but he remained by the pool, kicking off his boots, rolling up his jeans and dangling his feet into the deep end of the pool.

As they walked away, Rose looked back at him. His broad shoulders were silhouetted by the early evening sun and, for some reason she just couldn't quite fathom, she felt disappointed to be walking away from him.

CHAPTER 4

They spent the evening eating and chatting on the terrace. Thomas flitted by every now and then but, largely, was busy preparing for the arrival of a German tour group the following day.

As the sun began to set and strings of fairy lights lit up the wooden railings and the canopy above them, he finally sat down opposite them and breathed a long, tired sigh.

"Busy day?" Katie, for once, was being sincere.

Thomas made a *pffft* sound and shook his head. "We're a bit short staffed. Waiting for some new volunteers to arrive."

"Volunteers?" Rose was finally beginning to feel more relaxed and, although the way Thomas looked at her was making her stomach feel twitchy and twirly, she had decided to push it aside, completely ignore it, and try to behave like a normal human being who was capable of making conversation.

Thomas reached out and grabbed a handful of olives from the bowl in the middle of the table. "Mmm. We take on fifteen volunteers every summer to help out with the peak season. They get free riding lessons, food, accommodation, something to put on their C.V."

"And you get summer staff with very little actual expense," Katie finished, sounding impressed.

"Yep." Thomas tossed an olive into the air and caught it between his teeth, then handed one to Katie.

"I never beat you at this," she muttered, taking her turn and failing miserably – the olive ending up perilously close to landing on an adjoining table. "Here, Rose, you try..."

Rose's immediate instinct was to refuse. But then she took a deep breath, grabbed a small black olive, and utterly shocked herself by catching it *first time* between her slightly gappy front teeth.

Thomas let out a whoop, patted her firmly between the shoulder blades and grinned at his sister. "Ha! You need to up your game Katie."

"Beginner's luck," Katie laughed, trying a further four times before giving up in a pretend-huff and going in search of coffee.

Still laughing, Rose leaned back in her chair and sighed. Then she glanced at Thomas and said, "Thank you for letting us stay here, Thomas. It's an amazing place."

Thomas' legs were stretched out in front of him, ankles crossed. He raised his arms and laced his fingers together behind his head, his elbows jutting out sideways. "It's great to have you here." He looked at her and his mouth turned up at the corner, crinkling into a smile. "I kind of wish Katie had brought you sooner."

"It took a bit of persuading I'm afraid," Rose replied, ignoring his not-so-subtle attempt at flirting.

"Ah, yes. You're not a fan of horses, are you?"

Rose shuffled in her seat. Just the mention of them made her feel anxious. "Not so much."

"How come?" Thomas moved his chair so it was angled towards her and draped one arm over the back of his chair, opening his chest to her in a way that a body language expert might say indicated openness and vulnerability but which Rose was pretty sure was designed to show off his muscles.

She shrugged and tucked her hair behind her ear. "It's silly."

"I'm sure it's not."

"I..." Rose shook her head. The rationale behind her distrust of horses was so innocuous, so small, so insignificant that it would sound absolutely ridiculous if she said it out loud. Especially to Thomas.

Thankfully, she was saved by Katie, who returned holding a tray of coffees.

Rose was certain she saw Katie's eyes narrow as she took in Thomas' change in position, the way he'd nudged closer to Rose, the way he was leaning beside her. Perhaps she noticed Rose's flushed cheeks too because she picked up her mug, tilted her head towards the cabins and said, "Why don't we take these back and light the fire pit?"

"Sure." Rose stood up.

Thomas did too. But as he reached for his mug, Katie said, "Ah, girl time. Sorry."

Thomas smiled, nodded, and sat back down. "Sure. See you girls tomorrow."

As they were walking away, he called after them, "Katie, there's a trek going out at ten a.m. if you're interested? And Rose, if you want a gentle induction..."

"We'll think about it!" Katie shouted back. "Night, Tommy."

Rose woke early. Ridiculously early.

She had barely slept. Instead, she had tossed and turned and tried to think of how she was going to get out of accepting Thomas' offer of a 'gentle induction' to horse riding without looking like an absolute idiot.

At five a.m, accepting she wasn't going to figure out an answer, she pulled on a baggy grey sweater and slipped out onto the patio.

They had stayed up until midnight, enjoying the

warm glow of the fire pit, talking about work and home and the complete lack of romance in their lives.

Katie had broken up with her long-term boyfriend Greg just a few months ago and was desperate to find someone new. She'd tried online dating, apps, speed dating – the lot. Rose, however, had accepted her fate as the perpetually single member of their friendship group a long time ago; she *hated* putting herself on display, she couldn't think of anything worse than a blind date, and she avoided pubs and bars at all costs. So, her only real outlet for meeting people was work.

"And, trust me, the guys I work with are *not* dating material," she'd informed Katie, shaking her head as she pictured the pool of single men from her office.

"There must be *someone*, Rose."

"Katie, I'm an accountant. You've met accountants before, right? They're hardly suave, sophisticated, charming..."

"And that's what you're after is it? Charming?" Katie had raised her eyebrow and peered at Rose over her coffee cup.

Now, remembering the look on Katie's face, Rose was almost certain that she'd been hinting at something – hinting at the fact that Rose seemed to be turning to jelly around her best friend's *charming* older brother.

But maybe Rose was just being paranoid, reading too much into it. Maybe the fact that Thomas' mere presence seemed to be making her heart skip a beat had unnerved her. It had been such a long time since anyone had made her feel that way but, then again, it had been a long time since anyone had looked at her the way Thomas did.

Rose sighed and tried to drag her mind back to the beauty of the ranch. On the horizon, the sun was just beginning to creep up into the sky, bringing with it a delicate orange hue. She breathed in slowly.

Back when they were in school, Thomas, although older, had been the same as her – geeky, unfashionable, a little bit of a loner. Rose had always felt comfortable around him.

With other friends, she'd dreaded being left alone with their older siblings because she felt so meek and awkward. But at Katie's house, talking to Thomas as he drifted in and out of the kitchen or the lounge had always been comfortable, easy – nice.

Now, though, Thomas had become one of the cool kids. He was everything that Rose normally avoided, because she knew it was out of her reach and because it made her feel inferior.

She was shy, plain, and scared of pretty much everything. Thomas was the opposite – confidence practically shimmered on his sun-kissed skin. And yet the way he looked at her... well, it was exactly as Katie had described; clearly, somehow, Thomas Goodwin had learned how to make women feel good. He had learned how to make them feel special with just a cheeky smile and an expertly-delivered gaze. He had learned how to effortlessly slip compliments into conversation and how to flirt *just* enough that it made your heart race but not enough to be too obvious.

Rose shook her head and folded her arms in front of her chest. She knew better than to be flattered by a guy like Thomas Goodwin. And she wasn't going to allow herself to be sucked into his orbit.

"Good morning." The voice came from nowhere and jolted Rose out of her interior monologue and back onto the patio of the cabin.

"Thomas?" It was as if her thoughts had summoned him. He had come, seemingly, from nowhere and was holding a small blue flask in each hand.

"I was on the way to the stables." He gestured to the path beyond the swimming pool, then shook one of the flasks at her. "Coffee?"

"You made me coffee?"

"Actually, it was for Chris – he's leading today's trek – but I won't tell him if you don't."

Rose smiled, took the flask and tried to ignore the fact that Thomas' eyes were almost sparkling in the morning sunlight – dark brown but with tiny flecks of amber that she hadn't noticed before.

"You're up early," he said, perching on the low stone wall that enclosed the patio and taking a sip from his flask.

Rose shrugged, as if it was no big deal. As if she hadn't

just been standing there mulling over how and why Thomas Goodwin had become so incredibly attractive.

"You know, Rose, if you don't want to get involved with the horses, that's absolutely fine." He dipped his head to meet her eyes. "I get it. I'm not going to force you."

Rose cleared her throat and wrapped her hands around the warmth of the flask. "Thanks, Thomas. It's silly. The whole thing is silly, I know it is. I just can't..."

"Hey." Thomas placed his palms firmly on the low flint wall that separated them and stopping her before her words started to trip nervously over one another. "You don't have to explain. This is your vacation. If all you want to do is relax by the pool–"

"The pool that you built with your own bare hands?"

"Yeah, the pool I built with my *super talented* bare hands." Thomas laughed and shook his head at himself. "Then that's absolutely fine by me."

"Thank you," Rose said, meeting his eyes. "Really, Thomas, thank you."

Thomas glanced back at the cabin, then looked at his watch. "Okay, I should go. Tell Katie I said good morning, and remind her the trek leaves at ten"

"Sure." Rose tugged at the hem of her sweater. Looking down at her fingernails, she added casually, "Will we see you at breakfast?"

"Afraid not." He tapped his flask. "Caffeine is my breakfast." Then he waved and strode off towards the stables.

Rose breathed out heavily and scraped her fingers through her hair. So much for not allowing herself to fall for Thomas' charms. He'd brought her a flask of coffee and it had turned her to goo. She needed to get a grip. She needed to remember that Thomas was:

a) Katie's brother and therefore strictly out of bounds.

b) A player, or a cad, or however you wanted to phrase it.

c) Totally out of her league.

She was repeating this list to herself over and over when Katie appeared from inside. Blinking at the sunlight, she looked quizzically at Rose's coffee.

"Thomas stopped by," Rose said. "He wanted to remind you about the trek."

Katie smiled. "Bless him. He's a pain, but he can be lovely sometimes." She took the coffee from Rose, clearly thinking Thomas had brought it for her, and leaned back against the wooden exterior of the cabin. "Will you be okay today?"

"When you're out riding? Of course. I've got a book and the sunshine and the swimming pool. What else do I need?"

Katie raised her eyebrows and slurped loudly from the flask. "Well, it's a shame there's not some handsome Italian fellow wandering around who shares your aversion to horses. If Thomas could start conjuring that sort of thing up for his guests, then the place really would be in demand."

Rose shook her head. "How many times do I have to tell you that I *like* being single?"

"Until I start actually believing you," Katie replied, grinning.

Rose rolled her eyes. But as she followed Katie back inside, for the first time in a long time, she began to wonder whether she really did mean what she said. Did she like being single? Or had she just gotten used to it?

And what was it about Thomas that had made her suddenly start questioning herself?

CHAPTER 5

or the next five days, Rose and Katie settled
into the perfect vacation rhythm.

They ate breakfast together up at the ranch house,
looking out at the splendour of the Tuscan countryside
and watching the horses exercise in the paddocks closest to
the cabins. From a distance, Rose almost found them
pleasant to look at. But the thought of venturing closer still
made her legs turn to jelly.

Then, after breakfast each morning, when Katie
headed off on a trek with one of the various tour groups
that were staying at the ranch, Rose took a walk.

She walked around the half-landscaped, half-wild
gardens that surrounded the main building and the cabins.
She wandered beside the vegetable patch, said good
morning to the chickens, then looped back through the

immaculately designed Italian garden – with big box hedges and a fountain in its middle – to fetch her swimming things. Then she spent the rest of the day by the pool reading, soaking up the summer sun.

It was quite possibly the most relaxed Rose had ever been, which surprised her. But she was always thrilled to see Katie appear again mid-afternoon and take up her place on a nearby lounger.

On the sixth day of their holiday, however, Katie didn't look her usual smiling self when she approached the swimming pool.

"Rose?" She sat down on the lounger beside Rose and leaned forwards onto her knees.

Rose lifted her sunglasses. Her friend's face was crumpled into an expression that said, *I need to talk to you, and it's not good.*

Katie was chewing her lower lip. She breathed in sharply through her nose.

"What is it? Has something happened?" Rose's heart began to twitch uncomfortably in her chest. She sat up and raised her knees up to her chest.

"I had a call from the practice." Katie sighed and visibly tried to relax her shoulders. "One of my patients is in trouble."

"Oh... I'm sorry." Rose scooted over to Katie's lounger and put her arm around her.

"Rose." Katie turned to her and suddenly spoke very

quickly, as if she needed to get the words out all at once. "I have to go home. This patient – he's in a real mess and the therapist covering for me just isn't getting through. You know I wouldn't even consider it if it wasn't serious."

"Of course." Rose felt her muscles loosen. She'd miss her relaxing days by the pool, but at least going home would mean no more having to avoid Thomas' ridiculous smile and that strange gurgling sensation she felt whenever she saw him in the distance. "Have you rearranged our flights? When do you want to leave?"

Katie blinked at her. Then shook her head. "Oh, no, Rose. I wouldn't even *think* about making you come back too. It's doing you so much good to be away from things. I can see how happy and relaxed you are."

"Honestly, Katie, I don't mind. And I'm not sure I want to stay here alone. I–"

Katie squeezed Rose's arm. "Rose, honestly, please stay. It'll be good for you. Plus..." She glanced over to the ranch house. "Tommy turned away paying customers to let us stay. He's usually booked out at this time of year. If we both leave, it will be a bit of a slap in the face for him."

Rose felt her stomach tighten. She hadn't really thought about it like that – hadn't considered the fact that Thomas had gone out of his way to accommodate them and, essentially, gifted them a vacation worth *a lot* of money.

"Oh, well, if you're sure it's okay for me to stay?" She tried to look excited.

"Of course!" Katie wrapped her arms around Rose's neck and squeezed her tightly. "I'm just so sorry to have to cut our vacation short. I was having such a great time."

"I was too," Rose whispered. "I was too."

Katie's cab arrived at six p.m. to take her back to Rome airport. Rose waved her off from the terrace then retreated back to their cabin and flopped down onto the bed. She had never been abroad alone before. She'd always holidayed in England – trips to the coast and the Lake District, renting small cottages or staying in B&Bs. And, suddenly, looking at the vacant twin-bed beside hers, she felt very, very lonely.

She was fighting the urge to cry when a tap-tap-tap on the patio doors forced her to sit up.

Slowly, she walked towards them, her bare feet breathing a sigh of relief as they came into contact with the cool brick floor. Somehow, even before she opened it, she knew who she would find on the other side.

"Thomas?"

"Hey, Rose. How you doing?"

Rose swallowed hard and looked down at her frumpy choice of clothing: ill-fitting jeans and a mustard-yellow tunic. "Feel a bit lost, to be honest." She surprised herself with her honesty.

Thomas smiled at her and glanced back towards the

ranch house. "Well, dinner's up in half an hour. I'll save you a seat."

Rose tried to smile but the thought of having to sit with the tanned, slender, long-blonde-haired riding instructors and handsome ranch hands made her feel nauseous. Back in school, they were the kind of kids she would avoid at all costs – the ones guaranteed to make fun of the way she dressed and talked, and how much she enjoyed doing homework. "I might just grab something and eat back here," she mumbled.

Thomas frowned and glanced back into the room. "Well, listen, I know our accommodation is top-notch but it's not 'eat in your room' good." He reached out to pat her shoulder and smiled, a little more softly this time. "I'll take care of you, I promise. Just think about it, okay?"

Rose nodded and promised she would, even though deep-down she'd already decided – no *way* was she going to brave dinner with Thomas and his friends. Not without Katie by her side.

No way.

An hour later, when Rose was certain everyone would be seated and wouldn't notice her sneaking in at the back to grab a take-away carton of food, she made her way up to the main house and entered the dining room via the side door.

The room was buzzing with excited chatter. Tour groups were mingling with single travellers, and everyone was tucking in to large plates of salad and pasta. A couple of people were filling cartons with food to take outside or to their rooms, so Rose slipped up beside them and quickly scooped herself some pesto, some spaghetti, and some tomatoes.

She was about to turn and head back outside when she felt someone lingering behind her.

"Glad you could join us." Thomas was smiling at her, purposefully ignoring the fact that she was clearly trying to take her food and leave. "Saved you a seat, just like I promised." He looked up at the large table over by the wide open doors that led onto the terrace.

"Oh." There was no way out of it. "Thanks."

Rose awkwardly swung her legs over the bench and squeezed in beside Thomas and a girl she didn't recognise.

"Rose, this is Fleur." Thomas leaned over her and tapped Fleur on the arm.

"Fleur, this is Rose. My little sister's best friend."

Fleur grinned, a huge bright smile that made her face light up. "So nice to meet you. I'm sorry Katie had to leave – I was looking forward to trekking with her." Fleur scooped a fork full of tagliatelle into her mouth, then added. "Do you ride?"

Rose looked down at her food, nudging it with her fork. "Not really," she muttered.

"Rose isn't a big fan of horses," Thomas said, smiling.

"My mission for the next week is going to be to cure her of her phobia."

Rose's eyes widened and she felt her throat twitch uncomfortably. She tried to laugh but it came out as more of an *eeek* sound.

Fleur laughed quietly and smiled at her. "Oh, seriously Rose, don't worry. Thomas is amazing with this kind of thing. Quite a few kids from local schools come here for therapy. Almost all of them come apprehensive and leave just totally in love with the horses."

"Therapy?" Rose asked, feeling a bit like a meerkat sticking its head out of the ground as she looked either side of her from Fleur to Thomas.

"Mmm." Fleur nodded.

"We do equine assisted therapy for young people," Thomas explained. "Mainly kids who have experienced some kind of trauma or loss and need help processing it."

"Katie never told me you did stuff like that here – I thought it was just riding lessons and trekking."

Thomas shrugged and reached out to pour himself a glass of water. "It started that way, but I guess it's in the Goodwin family genes to help people." He chuckled. "Katie probably didn't mention it because she likes people to think she's the only sibling with a big heart."

Rose smiled and tried to shrug off the sense of almost-embarrassment that had settled in her stomach. People used horses for therapy – to help them overcome trauma – and yet she was scared of them for no particular reason.

"Don't worry," Thomas said, catching her eye. "I won't force you to mix with the horses if you really don't want to. This is your vacation. You didn't come here to be indoctrinated into our way of life."

Rose felt her chest loosen as she realised that Thomas was serious – he had no intention of making her do anything she wasn't ready for. "Thank you. I promise I'll think about it."

Thomas nodded at her and looked like he was about to say something else. But before he could, someone on the other side of the room shouted his name and waved at him.

"Thomas? A word?"

Thomas was already standing up, leaving his food half-eaten. "Rose, I'll catch you later. Got to run."

Rose lifted her hand and gave a small wave, then quickly tucked it back into her lap. Now that there was an empty space where Thomas had been, she felt unsteady and uncomfortable. She turned to Fleur, trying to think of something to say, but Fleur was deep in conversation with the girl opposite her.

For a moment, Rose sat eating her food and sipping her water in silence. But then, keenly aware that she was the only one in the room not talking to anyone, she took out her phone, tried to make it look like she'd received an interesting text or missed call, and retreated to the terrace with her carton of pasta.

She stood for a moment, looking out at the ranch. Although Thomas said he encouraged non-horsey people to visit and enjoy the surroundings, it was mostly full of visitors who were there for one purpose only – to ride. And now, without Katie to keep her company, Rose felt utterly out of her depth.

She didn't want to take Thomas up on his offer to help her overcome her fear of horses. She wanted to be left to her own devices, to spend the rest of her time at the ranch reading and sunbathing and counting down the days until she would return home.

But she also didn't want to become known as the 'weird girl who hated horses'. She imagined the other guests watching her swim and lounge and stay far away from the paddocks and the stables, and pictured them rolling their eyes and laughing at her behind her back.

Rose sighed. She thought she'd outgrown this. She thought that as an adult she would no longer find herself in uncomfortable situations. As an adult, you were supposed to be in control – able to decide who and what you interacted with.

But, somehow, she'd found herself in a position where her only choice seemed to be to either stand out like a sore thumb by sticking to her guns and avoiding the equine side of the ranch, or to come face-to-face with one of her biggest fears.

Either way, it wasn't going to be much of a vacation.

Telling herself an evening walk might clear her head, and that perhaps she could just take a *look* at the horses to see how she reacted, Rose set off past the trees, the lawn, and the swimming pool, and down the wide, curving, grey stone track that would eventually lead to the U-shaped stables and the sprawling fields of *Heart of the Hills* ranch.

Rose walked deliberately slowly, paying attention to the trees and the darkening sky, breathing in the scent of the Tuscan countryside and persuading herself not to think about where she was headed.

At least, now that most of the guests were inside eating, no one would notice if she bottled it and broke out in a cold sweat before getting anywhere close to a horse.

As she neared the stables, her heart started to tremble.

In the distance, the path stopped and became the stable yard on one side and fenced-in fields on the other. Towards the far end of the closest field, Rose could see the silhouettes of at least five horses grazing beneath the trees.

She had stopped and was about to turn around when she heard something. She narrowed her eyes, as if it would help her to hear better, and tried to focus.

At first, she thought it was a horse, an angry horse, a horse that had escaped and was about to charge towards her at break-neck speed.

But then she realised it was a person.

Rose glanced back towards the main building. Perhaps she should run and fetch someone. She was still lingering in the middle of the path when the noise grew louder.

"Help! I need help!"

"Thomas..." Rose breathed. And then, before she had a chance to stop herself, she found she was running. Except, she wasn't running away from the stables. She was running *towards* them.

CHAPTER 6

*R*ose stopped at the wooden gates that separated the yard from the track. She couldn't see anyone, but there was light coming from one of the stalls. Gingerly, she pushed the gate open. As she stepped through, it closed with a sharp sudden thud that made her jump.

Her feet didn't want to move. They prickled as if she could feel every grain of gravel beneath the soles of her shoes.

"Hello?! Anyone? *Aiuti!*" Thomas' voice called again, louder this time.

Rose breathed in sharply, closed her eyes, opened them, then ran towards the sound.

As she reached the stall that Thomas' voice had come from, she stopped and found herself bracing her arms against either side of the doorframe, as if she was a vampire unable to cross the threshold.

"Thomas?"

Thomas was on the floor. With the light outside waning, he was using a portable lamp to see and it was casting large exaggerated shadows on the walls. In front of him, a huge chestnut-brown horse was lying on its side, snorting heavy breaths from its nostrils.

The air was thick with the smell of horses and hay and it made Rose wrinkle her nose.

Thomas looked up. "Rose?" His cheeks were flushed and there was a film of sweat clinging to his forehead. He looked behind her, his eyes wide and searching. "Are you alone?"

"I heard you shouting. I was walking..." She trailed off and swallowed hard as the horse huffed loudly and shook its head at her. "What's happening?" she said, taking a few steps backwards.

"She's in labour." Thomas had one hand on the horse's stomach now and was stroking her nose with the other. "The foal is breech."

"The wrong way up?" Rose shuddered and looked back towards the path. "I'll go fetch help."

Thomas shook his head. "There's no time. The foal needs to come out now."

A cold, almost sea-sick feeling washed over Rose's arms and legs. She felt like she needed to sit down. The horse was trying to stand but Thomas was whispering to it to keep still.

"Rose, I can't keep her calm and deliver the foal. I need you at her head, I need you to talk to her."

"Talk to her?" Rose could barely get the words out. "What about?" It was a stupid question and, in other circumstances, Thomas might have laughed at it. But he didn't.

"Just talk calmly and slowly, she'll feel better in the dark so I'll move the light down this end. Just be with her, all right?"

Rose looked behind her, as if someone else may have magically appeared to take her place.

"Rose," Thomas was nodding at her. "You can do this." He looked at the mare and then back at Rose. "We need you to do this."

Rose breathed in slowly through her nose, then shook her head. If she'd have been wearing sleeves, she would have rolled them up as she found herself saying, "Right. Okay. Right..." and kneeling down beside the panting horse.

"Her name is Delilah," Thomas said, moving backwards and positioning himself behind the horse's tail. "That's it, Delilah, this is Rose. She's going to be your birthing partner and I'm going to be down the business end getting things sorted out."

Rose sat down, the hay prickling at her legs as she tucked them beneath her. With trembling fingers, she reached out. Delilah puffed at her and Rose immediately took her fingers back. Her heart was beating so fast she thought she might be descending into a panic attack. But then Delilah moved her head and looked at Rose. She had deep brown eyes and long thick eyelashes.

"Oh," Rose breathed. "She's so scared."

Thomas looked up. "Talk to her," he nudged.

Rose nodded at him, deliberately trying not to see what he was doing to help the foal out of its mother.

"Delilah, I'm Rose." She shuffled forwards. And, this time, when Delilah puffed and rocked her head, Rose only flinched a little. "It's okay," she said. "It's going to be okay. Thomas is taking such good care of you and your baby."

Delilah looked at her and blinked slowly.

"Beautiful girl," Rose murmured. "It's all right. It's all going to be all right."

"Okay," said Thomas, urgently. "I'm going to turn the foal now. Keep her calm, Rose. Yeah?"

Rose swallowed hard. She nodded. And as Delilah whinnied and puffed and sweat glazed her back and her flanks, Rose started to sing. She didn't know where it came from. It just started – a sweet, gentle melody that her mum sang to her when she was a baby.

Thomas was struggling. Rose could see him from the corner of her eye, but she didn't take her gaze from Delilah's – just kept on singing, again and again, the same verse. Until Thomas shouted, "Got it! Okay, okay Rose, back away."

Rose looked at him. "I... are you sure?"

"She can do the rest." Thomas was standing up and moving towards the door, beckoning for Rose to follow him.

Slowly, she got up and backed away.

And what seemed like only seconds later, suddenly, there was a foot... another foot... a head... a foal. A gangly, dark brown foal.

Rose felt her hands fly to her mouth.

She looked at Thomas. He was grinning. "That's it, Dee. That's it."

"Look at him." Rose had never truly felt awe-struck in her entire life. But gazing at the tiny horse in front of her, with a white diamond splash on its nose and sticky-up ears, she could barely speak.

Thomas had cleaned himself off and borrowed Rose's phone to call the vet. Now, he was standing with his arms crossed, smiling as Delilah gently licked her baby's legs. Unfolding his arms, he put one of them around Rose's shoulders and pulled her in close. "That wasn't quite how I pictured curing you of your phobia."

Rose laughed and looked up at him. His arm felt heavy and warm and she was about to lean into him when she heard someone behind them yell, "Thomas! Thomas, what happened?!"

Turning around, Rose saw Fleur jumping over the gate and running towards them.

Immediately, Thomas' arm dropped to his side and he turned, his face animated but his voice hushed as he told Fleur about the foal.

Fleur hadn't even looked at Rose yet but when Thomas said, "Thankfully, Rose was passing and did a pretty amazing job of keeping Dee calm," she turned and smiled.

"Rose?" Fleur wrinkled her brow, as if she'd already forgotten who she was. "Oh, Rose?! But you're scared of horses?"

"Not any more, she's not," Thomas said smoothly, nudging Rose in the ribs.

Rose peered into the stable and looked at Delilah. She didn't feel scared of *this* horse anymore. But she still couldn't imagine coming face-to-face with another one and the idea that Thomas might expect her to be magically cured and ready to go riding made her stomach begin to cramp.

"Well, that's great," said Fleur. "Well done." Then she turned back to Thomas. "Is Rossi on his way?"

Thomas nodded and glanced up at the sky. It was almost dark. "Should be here soon, but I think Dee's okay."

"I'll wait with you." Fleur put her hand on Thomas's shoulder and, for some reason, it made Rose feel uncomfortable.

She cleared her throat. "I'll see you guys tomorrow."

"Sure," said Thomas, patting her arm. "There's no need to stay now. The hard part's done. You were great, Rose. Thank you."

"No problem." Her words came out a little too quickly. "See you."

But Thomas had already turned back to Fleur.

Walking back towards her cabin, Rose sighed and patted at her frizzy brown hair. Fleur had big blue eyes and long blonde hair. She was tanned, confident, and had legs up to her armpits. Beside her, Rose felt plain and mousy. And the way Fleur had looked at Thomas, for some reason, it bothered Rose. It niggled at her and made her skin feel too tight and too hot.

There was no reason it should. Thomas, and who Thomas dated, was nothing to do with her.

Rose shook her head and then breathed in sharply through her nose. Thomas Goodwin was out of her league. And, besides, he was Katie's brother. He was out of bounds. Out. Of. Bounds. And all this mooning around after him wasn't going to do her any good at all.

CHAPTER 7

The next morning, Rose woke to the sound of something tapping on the patio doors. Slowly, rubbing her eyes and squinting at the light sneaking in from around the curtains, she slid out of bed, shuffled her feet into her sandals, and pulled a cardigan over her pyjamas.

At first, when she opened the curtains, she didn't see anything. But then she noticed a little blue flask sitting on the wall. Stepping outside, she moved gingerly towards it, as if someone might jump out and say 'boo'.

There was no one there, but tucked underneath the flask was a note that read:

Thanks for your help last night, Remarkable Rose. I'll be going to see Delilah and the foal at eight thirty. Meet by the pool?

Rose's fingers tightened around the note.

Last night, adrenaline had taken over. She hadn't had time to think about how scared she was. But now, in the cold light of the morning, she wasn't sure she could do it. What if she got within two feet of Delilah and freaked out? Thomas would think she was crazy. And, despite what she kept telling herself, she liked that last night he had seen a different side of her. A side that wasn't just mousy and timid. She didn't want to ruin it by having a meltdown in front of him.

Breathing in deeply, she took the flask back inside and sat on the bed. Sipping at the now lukewarm coffee, she picked up her phone. A message from Katie was waiting for her.

So sad I'm not waking up in our little cabin this morning. Hope you're okay and that Tommy is looking after you. K xxx

Rose's thumbs lingered over the keyboard. Eventually, she replied:

All good. Miss you but Thomas being nice. I helped him deliver a foal last night! Hope all is okay with your patient. xx

Rose held her phone for a while, watching the screen to see if Katie would reply. It was almost eight when it started to ring.

"You delivered a foal?!" Katie's voice was both animated and disbelieving at the same time.

Rose laughed. "Well, Thomas did the delivering part. But I sat with Delilah and kept her calm."

"I'm sorry, how long have I been gone?"

Rose pictured Katie shaking her head and frowning.

"When I left yesterday morning, my friend Rose was terrified of horses and now – less than twenty four hours later – she's cured? Not only cured... delivering baby horses?!"

Rose laughed and shook her head. "I'm definitely *not* cured. I was just taking a walk and..." As she regaled Katie with what had happened, Rose realised she was feeling different from normal – proud, almost. Usually, she downplayed her achievements. She wasn't the sort of person who told amusing stories or captured peoples' attention the way Katie and Thomas did when they spoke. But as she told Katie about sitting beside Delilah and singing to her, and how the foal had just come straight out and tried to stand up, and how amazing it had been, she heard something new in her voice. Something that she actually quite liked.

"Rose. That's amazing. I'm so proud of you! I just can't believe I wasn't there."

"Well, to be honest," Rose said, "if you were here, I wouldn't have done it, would I? I'd have just hung back and let you help."

"Wow, so it turns out that me leaving was actually just what you needed?" Katie chuckled.

"I guess so." Rose laughed but then she added, "I do miss you, though. I've no idea what I'm going to do all day.

Thomas asked me to go with him and check on Delilah but I'm not sure."

"Rose, you have to go." Katie was speaking very sternly. "You have to keep the momentum going. If you retreat to your comfort zone, you'll just go right back to being scared. But if you face it – you could actually come home having overcome your fear, which is a *huge* deal. And I know I warned Thomas to stay away from you, but he really is amazing with the horses. If anyone can help you, he can." Katie paused and laughed. "Just remember – don't fall for his charms. I know he's wonderful and, as weird as it is for me to say, pretty good looking. But he's a disaster with relationships. I don't want you to get hurt."

"I'm not exactly looking for a relationship, Katie." Rose prickled at the implication that she couldn't possibly just have a bit of harmless fun. That, of course, she would fall in love and get too attached and her heart would end up shattered into millions of pieces. She was about to say so, when she glanced up at the clock. "Katie, I have to go. It's nearly eight thirty. If I'm going to go see Delilah–"

"Of course, go. And Rose?"

"Yes?"

"I'm really proud of you."

The prickle subsided and Rose smiled. "Thanks, Katie. I'll text you later."

It was eight thirty-five when Rose jogged towards the swimming pool. But Thomas was still waiting for her. He smiled as she approached, raising his hand to shield his eyes from the sun and grinning his trademark grin.

"You got my note. Thought you might have slept in..."

"Unlikely, when someone was tapping on my doors at seven a.m."

"Not tapping," Thomas said matter-of-factly. "Throwing stones, actually."

"Oh, stones. Just what everyone wants to wake up to on their vacation."

"I did bring you coffee though."

Rose smiled. "You did. Thank you."

"And you decided to brave a visit to Delilah?"

Rose breathed in deeply and tried to make the muscles in her shoulders relax. "I did."

Thomas reached out and put his hand on her forearm. "It'll be okay, Rose."

She blushed and looked up at him then, as they started walking towards the stables, she said, "I know it's silly..."

"Hey," he replied, looking at her sternly. "It's not *silly*. Stop saying that. Plenty of people are afraid of things. Heck, I'm scared of cats."

"Cats?" Rose wrinkled her forehead at him. "You're scared of cats?"

"Okay, well not *scared* of them. But I definitely don't trust them." Thomas glanced at her from the corner of his eye and Rose stifled a laugh.

"Right. Not quite the same thing."

"No, but seriously, it's nothing to be embarrassed about, Rose."

Rose could tell she was starting to blush. Her neck was always the first to turn pink; her pale skin becoming blotchy and flushed. "Thank you."

Softly, Thomas added, "Was there something that triggered it?"

Rose laughed wryly and shook her head. "That's the ridiculous thing. There's nothing. Nothing I can remember. I've always just found horses so... intimidating. Powerful. *Big*."

"Okay, so maybe we'll get you started with a little horse," Thomas said, nudging her gently with his elbow.

Rose sighed. She was finding it hard to smile. "I guess I've just always been so wary of things." She shrugged and shook her head. "Probably my parents' fault. Maybe they mollycoddled me or something. Never let me fall down or play in wet clothes or eat dirt."

Thomas made a mock-outraged expression and tutted loudly. "Didn't allow you to eat dirt? How dare they?"

"You met my parents, right?" Rose's family had spent several summer afternoons hanging out with Katie and Thomas' parents. Although Rose always remembered Thomas slinking away inside to play on his X-box.

"Sure. They're great. Although I do remember your mum being slightly... over cautious."

Rose nodded fervently. "Yes. Just a bit."

"Well, I was hardly Mister Confidence back then. Don't you remember?" Thomas looked at her quickly, then looked away. Was he blushing? Surely not?

Rose shrugged. She did remember. But Thomas was so different now that he seemed like an entirely new person.

Thomas shook his shoulders, as if he was physically shooing away the memory. "Anyway, listen. My point is – being nervous or afraid is nothing to be embarrassed about. Okay?"

"Okay."

When they reached the paddock opposite the stable yard, Thomas paused and rested his hand on the gate. "Ready?"

Rose was not ready. She could see Delilah and the foal standing beneath a tree at the far end of the paddock. From here, they looked harmless, beautiful even. But she still felt sick to her stomach at the thought of walking towards them. "Yep. Ready."

Thomas unlatched the gate. Then, as they stepped through, he took Rose's hand in his.

He squeezed it, gently. And it was like all the nerves and the anxiety she was feeling started to melt away. The warmth of his fingers around hers spread through her limbs and, even though her heart was still pounding, the nausea that a few moments ago had threatened to overwhelm her, disappeared.

"Did I mention that you look nice today?" Thomas asked, smiling cheekily at her as they strode through the grass towards the trees.

"Is that your way of trying to distract me?"

"Maybe," he laughed. "Did it work?"

"No," she said, looking down at her denim shorts and pale green T-shirt. "Not even a little bit."

As they approached Delilah, Rose tried to remember the night before. When the horse had been lying on its side, looking into Rose's eyes... vulnerable... scared.

Slowly, Delilah turned to look at her. She made a little *huff* sound and started to walk towards them. As she did, Rose stopped and gripped Thomas' arm.

"It's okay. She's coming to say hello. That's all."

Thomas reached out and stroked Delilah's nose. Behind her, her foal wobbled over to them on thin, bandy, not quite steady legs.

Rose smiled at the tiny horse. "I think he's more my kind of size," she said, looking at Thomas.

"Adorable, huh?" Thomas bent down and reached out his hand. The foal tottered towards it and Rose looked nervously up at Delilah.

"Will she mind?"

"Not a bit," Thomas replied, softly. Then, to the foal, he said, "Hey buddy, this is Remarkable Rose. She pretty much saved your life."

Rose blushed and shook her head. "I absolutely didn't. That was you."

"But without you, I wouldn't have been able to. So..." Thomas paused and beckoned for Rose to bob down beside him. "I was thinking that maybe you should name him."

"Really?" Rose was reaching out her fingers but they weren't shaking the way she'd expected them to. And when she touched the foal's nose and stroked the little splash of white that had formed a perfect diamond shape, she smiled. "How about Piccolo?"

Thomas' brow wrinkled. "I didn't know you spoke Italian?"

"I don't." Rose shook her head. "I played the piccolo in high school. Don't you remember? I was one of the band geeks who got wheeled out at assembly time to serenade everyone."

Thomas laughed, tipping his head back a little. "Ha, actually I *do* remember. The piccolo is the tiny flute, right?"

"That's the one."

"Well, it's perfect. In Italian it means 'little'."

"I know." Rose was still stroking the foal's nose, marvelling at how calm and trusting he was and how incredible it was that Delilah was just letting them stand there, so close to her baby.

"Okay," said Thomas. "Piccolo it is."

When they returned to the ranch, Thomas headed to the office to call Rossi the vet and update him on the foal, and Rose went to change into her swimming costume.

Deciding to go for green instead of the black version that she'd worn every day since she and Katie arrived, she pulled it on, threw a kaftan over the top, ditched her phone by the bed, and headed outside.

Today, the pool was busier than usual. Perhaps because it was later in the day, perhaps because the ranch was getting more populated as it drew closer to the peak of the season.

Rose chose a lounger in the corner, away from the others, put her towel and her book on top of it, discarded her kaftan, then dove straight into the water.

Usually, she would sit on the edge of the pool and ease herself in inch-by-inch. But today, she submerged her whole body in one go. The shock of the cool water made her gasp but when she emerged, she was grinning.

She did it. She confronted her fear and nothing terrible happened. Delilah was gentle and soft and, yes, big and powerful. But not *scary* and big and powerful. And Piccolo... well, she didn't think even *she* could manage to be afraid of him.

So, maybe, just maybe, Katie was right; being alone at the ranch, with Thomas, could be the best thing that had ever happened to her.

CHAPTER 8

*L*ater that evening, Rose snuck her dinner away
from the ranch house and ate on her patio,
looking out over the small flint wall at the pool
and the horses in the distance. She had intended to eat
with Thomas and Fleur at the big 'cool kids' trestle table –
swallow her nerves and make herself find something interesting to say – but when she arrived, neither Thomas or
Fleur was there.

She had briefly met some of the other trainers and
instructors, but definitely didn't know them well enough
to just walk up there and sit down. So, telling herself it
was probably a sign that she should take some time away
from Thomas, she retreated to the cabin and ate alone,
mulling over everything that had happened since Katie
had left.

When the sun began to set, a chill crept into the air, so

Rose fetched the fire lighting kit from inside and, after several failed attempts, lit the fire pit.

She was sitting beside it, texting Katie to tell her about her encounter with Delilah and marvelling at how clear the sky was above the ranch, when she spotted a shadowy figure walking towards her.

It was almost dark. Stars were beginning to flicker in the sky above her and, although she immediately recognised his broad shoulders and his confident stride, Rose waited until Thomas was right in front of her before saying, "Not more coffee?"

He was holding a customary flask in each hand and tilted his head as he said, "Hot chocolate, actually." He offered her one, then hopped over the wall and sat down beside her in the chair that usually belonged to Katie.

Rose tugged a blanket from the back of her chair and draped it over her knees, snuggling down a little and wrapping her hands around the warmth of the flask. "Don't you have any other friends?" she asked, surprising herself by making fun of him.

Thomas, clearly surprised too, laughed loudly and shook his head at her. "I guess not." Then, a little more seriously, he added, "It's kinda tough being the boss *and* having friends, you know."

"I'm sorry, I was just..." Rose began to blush awkwardly; she hadn't meant to offend him.

"I know." Thomas grinned at her. "I'm just messing with you, Rose."

"Sorry," she said again, sipping her drink and looking up at the sky. "I'm not so good with banter."

"Oh, I'd say you're okay."

"Only okay?"

"Maybe we'll work on it after we've worked on your horse phobia."

Rose involuntarily shuddered. "You're not giving up on that, huh?"

Thomas took the lid off his drink and blew at it to cool it down. "I will if you want me to. But, honestly, you were pretty amazing last night. And today – you smashed it."

Rose laughed self-consciously and tucked her hair behind her ear. "I'm not sure–"

"Are you kidding? Of course you did. *Smashed* it." Thomas made a 'slam-dunk' gesture with his left arm then settled back into his chair, stroking his beard thoughtfully. "I really don't think it will take much to get you feeling more confident. Maybe even get you on a trek?" He raised his eyebrows at her as he said 'trek' but when Rose visibly recoiled, he lifted his hand at her and said, "Okay, okay, maybe trekking is too far."

Rose shuffled in her chair so that she was angled towards him. "What did you have in mind? To *cure* me?"

"Nothing too traumatic, I promise. Some time with Delilah and the foal again tomorrow, then maybe a couple of the others the day after. *Small* horses, very small, and dainty." Thomas made an 'I'm being very serious' face, then looked into the flames of the fire pit. "To be honest, I think even just watching them and spending time getting to know them would do wonders for you. With Delilah, you got it. As soon as you looked into her eyes, you saw her soul. And that's what they do – horses – they get you here..." Thomas thumped his chest, above his heart. "That's how they got me." He looked around at the cabins either side of them and the fields in the distance. "That's why I'm still here – nearly fifteen years after I first arrived."

"Fifteen years?" Rose frowned, trying to do the maths. "Wow, so you're *thirty-six*?"

Thomas gave her a quizzical look. "There's no need to say it like that – I've a fair while to go before I'm put out to pasture."

Rose laughed. A short bubble of a laugh that made her snort into her drink.

The snort made Thomas laugh too, and Rose covered her mouth with her hand, aware that if she *really* started to laugh she'd snort even more.

"Stop it," she said, waving him away. "I just meant that I'm surprised so much time has passed, that's all. And I never realised you were five years older than us."

"Yes. Five years. Older and wiser." Thomas finished his hot chocolate and put the flask down on the floor between his feet, leaning forwards and opening his palms at the fire. "I didn't see you at dinner," he added, quietly. The simmering cheekiness that usually danced on his lips had faded and he looked at Rose from the corner of his eyes, not quite turning to face her.

"I didn't see you either," she said, trying not to make it sound as if she'd been looking for him.

"You like being alone?" Thomas was watching her intently.

"*Like* it?" Rose bit her lower lip and nursed her flask between her hands. "I'm not sure I *like* it. I'm just used to it. And when I'm around lots of people, I get a bit... nervous." She sighed a little and sipped her drink. "I've always wished I could be more like Katie – bright and confident and just not phased by things."

"You know what I think?" Thomas raised his eyebrows at her, smiling beneath his beard. "I think that you are great just as you are. You don't need to try and be someone else, Rose. You're great. Really great." He laughed and shook his head. "Wow, I just said 'great' a fair few times, didn't I?"

"You did," she smiled.

"Well, you are. So..." Thomas suddenly stood up, clearing his throat and rubbing the back of his neck as if he wasn't really sure what to say next.

"So..."

"I should get going. One last check on Dee and the foal then bed."

"Okay, well, thank you for the hot chocolate." Rose reached up to offer him the flask back and for just the smallest flash of a second, their fingertips brushed against one another. The contact made her flinch, and she stood up quickly.

Thomas was close to her and the blanket had fallen to the floor between them. Rose folded her arms in front of her chest. Her brain was whirring. She was trying to think of something witty to say. Or at least something that would distract her from the fact that Thomas was still looking at her, still tracing her features with his gaze in a way that made her legs feel like they were about to buckle.

But before she could, he put the flasks down on the wall, hopped back over it, picked them up again and said, "I'll see you in the morning."

Rose nodded. Did he mean that he'd bring her coffee in the morning? Or was he just saying, *See you in the morning*? "Sure," she said, stepping forwards and closer to the warmth of the fire pit. "See you tomorrow, Thomas."

CHAPTER 9

The following morning, Rose woke at six. She had set her alarm, which seemed ridiculous because she was on vacation and supposed to be having endless lie-ins, but something told her that Thomas would be back. And, for once, she didn't really want to greet him with bed-hair and her customary scruffy pyjamas.

She also, however, didn't want to make it look like she'd set her alarm. Because then it would seem like she wanted to impress him. And she didn't. Or, at least, she didn't want him to think that she did.

Sighing, because her tumbling, mixed up thoughts were starting to make her feel crazy, she went to the bathroom, splashed water on her face, combed her hair with her fingers so it was more 'tousled' and less 'bird's nest', then put on a very light coating of tinted moisturiser.

Back in the bedroom, she switched her oversized white

sleep shirt for a black vest top and shrugged on her woolly grey cardigan.

Looking in the mirror, she was satisfied that she looked better than normal but not so much better that it would be obvious to Thomas that she'd just applied makeup and brushed her hair.

Then, she sat on the edge of the bed and waited for the tap-tapping.

She'd almost given up and was about to slump back under the sheets and go back to sleep, when she heard it. *Tap, tap tap tap.*

Slowly, slower than she wanted to, she got up and nudged open the curtains.

Thomas was scribbling a note on a piece of paper but when he looked up, he saw her and grinned.

Rose opened the door and stepped outside into the crisp morning air. "Do you offer this service to all your guests?" she asked – she'd been planning that since she'd woken up.

"Only the ones I like," Thomas replied, smoothly.

The comment surprised her; she hadn't expected him to answer like that and it stopped her in her tracks.

"Plus, I've got to look after my sister's best friend, haven't I?" Thomas added, quickly, as if he felt like he needed to quantify the term 'like'.

Rose took the flask of coffee that he'd put on the wall and made a 'cheers' gesture. "Well, it's very much appreciated. Thank you. And I'll tell Katie that you're doing a brilliant job."

Thomas smiled. He was lingering, holding his own coffee as if he wasn't really sure whether he should stay or go.

"So, what's on your agenda today?" Rose asked, leaning against the cold flint wall.

Thomas made a *pffft* sound that reminded Rose of Delilah. "Well," he said, rubbing at his beard as if he was trying to remember his schedule. "A lot, actually. We've got a couple of small groups arriving this morning and three treks going out. I'm leading the first one in..." he glanced at his watch, "about an hour's time."

"Where do you go on these treks?" Rose asked, looking up at the hills in the distance.

"Depends on the level of the riders. This one's an advanced one, so we'll be out all day. But I was thinking, why don't you just come down and watch us getting the horses ready? You don't have to get too close. You can sit under a tree and just *observe*." Thomas smiled temptingly and it made Rose's breath catch in her chest.

"Won't people think I'm..."

"Think you're...?" Thomas shook his head at her, as if he had no idea what she was trying to say.

"Odd. Weird. You know, coming to a ranch and not riding."

Thomas chuckled softly and reached out to touch her hand. "Rose, I mean this in the nicest possible way – no one will pay you any attention. Everyone will be too busy focussing on what they're doing to wonder why you're not riding."

Rose was chewing the inside of her cheek and must have looked horribly worried because Thomas dipped his head to meet her eyes and smiled at her. "I guess..." she paused, took a deep breath, then said, "Okay, sure. Okay."

"Great!" Thomas beamed. "I'll go up to the ranch house, check they're geared up for the arrivals, then swing back here and collect you. Okay?"

"Okay."

"You'll be fine, Rose. See you soon."

Rose waved and watched Thomas jog up to the ranch house. Yesterday, she'd gone with him because she believed Katie was right – it would be good for her to face her fear and try to overcome it.

Today, she was pretty sure that was *not* the reason she'd agreed to go and watch Thomas and the other riders prepare for their trek. The idea filled her with dread. She already felt twitchy and self-conscious at the thought of being the odd one out – just standing there and watching everyone else.

Today, she'd said yes because Thomas wanted her to. Because last night, she had felt like there was something between them. Something dancing in the air, almost said but not quite. And although the sensible, protective part of her brain was telling her that this was exactly what guys like Thomas did – compliments and smouldering looks and almost-touches – she just couldn't match the Thomas she was spending time with to the Thomas that Katie had warned her about.

He seemed genuine. And the only way she'd find out for sure, would be to spend more time with him.

So, despite the voice in her head that was yelling, *Just stay away from him, Rose,* she went back inside, showered, dressed, and waited for Thomas to come back for her.

As they approached the stable yard and the paddock where she'd met Delilah and Piccolo, Thomas reached out and squeezed Rose's hand in his. He stopped and gestured to some trees. Beneath them was a picnic bench.

"Why don't you wait there?"

Rose looked from Thomas to the bench. She didn't really want to let go of his hand, but waiting out of the way under the trees seemed like something she could handle. "Okay."

"Just watch and when you've seen enough, head back up and relax by the pool. Yeah?"

Rose nodded. She felt a bit queasy. She wanted to ask just how many horses would be going on this trek, but she also didn't really want to hear the answer because it would make her want to run straight back up to the ranch house.

So, she did as Thomas suggested; she went and sat at

the picnic bench, put her sunglasses on so that she could avoid looking at people, and watched as Thomas and some helpers she didn't recognise started to bring horses, one by one, out of the stables.

The horses were lined up and tied to a series of posts a bit further down from where Rose was sitting. Most of them were a little smaller than Delilah, sandy brown with light coloured manes. They all seemed very calm. Occasionally, one would whinny or snort, but mostly they stood patiently and quietly, waiting.

Slowly, as Rose watched them, the sea-sick feeling in her stomach began to subside. Behind her, a group of six riders were making their way down the path from the ranch house, chattering excitedly, all dressed in jeans and riding boots.

They waved at her and said good morning as they passed, which surprised Rose. She had been looking down at her phone, trying to make it seem as if she was absorbed in something, but when she looked up she waved back, and smiled, and again some of her nerves dissipated.

The riders gathered in front of the horses and, as she watched Thomas issue instructions for the trek, Rose tried not to smile. She kept catching herself laughing at something he said or smiling when he caught her eye.

He was so at ease in his own skin – a feeling Rose had *never* had – and the way he spoke, with such confidence and knowledge, *almost* made her want to get up and run over and ask if she could join them.

He was wearing his red boots and as the other riders mounted their horses, he took a similarly cowboy-esque hat from a nearby post and planted it swiftly on his head.

"Okay guys, great, if you head over through that gate and into the field at the end of the path, I'll follow you."

The riders began to file slowly away from Rose and the picnic bench, towards the gate. The clip-clop of the horses' hooves was slow and gentle, and Rose was surprised by just how easy it all seemed.

"You okay?" Thomas bobbed down in front of her and rested his arms on the table, watching her carefully.

"I'm good," she said, smiling.

"Really?" Thomas clearly thought she was trying to be brave.

"Really. I feel fine. It was nice, actually." Rose looked over Thomas' shoulder towards the field where the riders were now gathered, waiting for him. "You better go," she said. "You're holding up the group."

Thomas laughed, nodded and stood up slowly, as if he didn't really want to go. But then he patted his hand on the table and said, "Right. Okay. Well done, Rose. You did really well. I'll see you later."

Turning away from her, he walked briskly over to a dark brown mare with a big white splodge on her back, mounted her in one swift movement, and trotted to where the other riders were patiently waiting.

Positioning himself at the front of the group, he waved

at Rose before setting off towards the track at the far end of the paddock that led away from the ranch.

Rose returned the gesture and waited until they were out of sight before she walked back to the ranch house, wondering just how long an 'all-day' trek lasted and whether she'd see Thomas that evening.

CHAPTER 10

*R*ose waited on the patio until ten p.m., when the fire pit began to fizzle out and she was pretty certain that Thomas would not be bringing her hot chocolate.

She was sure she'd seen some of the riders who'd been on the trek eating dinner on the terrace when she'd ventured up to the ranch house for dinner. And she'd even forced herself to sit and eat with Fleur and the others, hoping that Thomas would appear.

But he hadn't.

And she hadn't dared to ask about him; if she did, her question would come out high-pitched and excited, making it plainly obvious that she had a giant crush on him.

Earlier that morning, she'd still been telling herself that the giddy, swoon-like feelings she got whenever she was close to Thomas were just the result of him being the only good-looking guy who'd so much as spoken to her, let alone paid her compliments, in a long, long time.

But now, heading back inside and sliding the patio doors closed behind her, she knew it was more than that.

She had spent the entire day thinking about him and every time she pictured him sauntering up to her in his silly hat and boots, she felt a nervous little bubble of excitement in her stomach. A bubble that told her this was not simply a case of feeling flattered by him or lonely because Katie had gone home.

She liked him. She liked talking to him and being around him. And she felt as if he liked being around her too. Which was both disastrous and exciting at the same time.

But now, when she'd expected him to come and tell her about his day, hop over her wall and sit beside her like he'd done the night before, he hadn't shown up.

They hadn't agreed that he would. They hadn't discussed it or made any arrangements, so she didn't really have any right to feel disappointed.

But she did.

And now she was wondering whether this was precisely what Katie had warned her about – becoming infatuated and, ultimately, ending up getting hurt.

As if her friend could read her mind, or had spy cameras in the cabin, Rose had only just slumped down on the bed and buried her head in her hands when a text from Katie lit up her phone.

How's it going? My patient is feeling much better, which is awesome, but also makes me miss you and the ranch.

Rose sighed and held the phone close to her chest. Normally, if she had a crush on someone – which hadn't happened for a *very* long time – Katie would be the first person she talked to. The person she'd ask for advice and who she'd analyse all the silly little details with: he looked at me like this; he spoke to me like that; I think he almost held my hand; gosh, he's so handsome.

But now, for the first time, she felt like there was a great big secret between them. And she didn't like it.

She wanted to reply and say, *Funny story, so you know how you told me absolutely NOT to fall for your brother? Well, the thing is, he's so good looking, and funny, and confident, and he makes me feel special, and I'm pretty sure I like him A LOT. That's cool? Right?*

But, of course, she didn't. She couldn't.

Firstly, Katie would be super-mad that Rose had ignored her advice and secondly, even if she wasn't mad, she'd tell Rose that Thomas was simply doing what he always did – flattering his way into a girl's heart before breaking it.

So, instead, Rose replied:

Miss you too. I'm getting better with the horses, didn't see Thomas much today as he was on a trek. I think he wants to get me doing one, but there's a long way to go before that happens!

Then she turned off her phone, crawled into bed, and tried to push all thoughts of Thomas Goodwin from her brain.

Tomorrow, she'd wake up and she'd shake it off. She'd treat him like a friend. Just a friend. Nothing more.

Just. A. Friend.

CHAPTER 11

*W*hen Rose woke, it was nine a.m. She hadn't bothered to set her alarm the night before and there had been no tap-tapping on the patio doors to wake her.

Gingerly opening the curtains, as if somehow there might still be a blue flask of coffee waiting for her, Rose let out a small resigned sigh.

She'd intended to wake up with a renewed resolve to put her guard back up and ignore Thomas' charms. And yet, she couldn't ignore the disappointed tug in her belly as she ventured outside and found no sign of him having come to see her.

Back inside, she dressed for the day – white cut-offs, a black vest top and a thin white cardigan – then ventured up towards the ranch house.

She'd missed breakfast. By now, all the riders would be

ready to set off for lessons and treks, so she headed for the coffee machine in the dining hall instead.

She was piling in three big spoons of sugar when Fleur sidled up beside her.

"Morning, Rose, how are you doing?"

"Good, thanks," she replied quietly. "How are you?"

Fleur yawned. "Bit of a late night actually. Delilah had some problems. Thomas and I had to call the vet out. Have you met Rossi? He's a really nice guy. Typical Italian – tall, dark, handsome."

Rose frowned, trying to sort the information into relevant categories. There were problems with Delilah – so *that* was why she hadn't seen or heard from Thomas.

"Is she okay?"

"She is now," Fleur nodded. "Thanks to Rossi."

Rose wanted to go and find Thomas, to ask what had happened and see if he was all right, but for some reason she didn't want Fleur to know that she was worried about him. "That's good," she said. "I'm glad she's all right."

Fleur smiled, then lingered for a moment as if she'd run out of things to say. "Okay, bye Rose. See you around."

Rose waved, shovelled another spoonful of sugar into her coffee, and took it out to the terrace. She had almost finished it, and was wondering whether to go for a walk or fetch her swimming things, when she felt a firm hand on her shoulder.

Instantly, a tingle of electricity shot from the top of her

head to the tips of her toes. She tried to turn around slowly. But she didn't quite manage it.

"Thomas... I saw Fleur. She said Delilah had to see the vet last night?"

Thomas looked tired. He had dark circles under his normally-bright eyes and his skin was paler than usual. But he was still smiling. "She's okay now, but it was a bit scary. I found her when I did my final checks at sun-down. She was in a bad way. An infection, we think. But Rossi gave her antibiotics and seems to have got it under control."

Rose smiled, relieved that Delilah was okay, but also relieved that there was a reason Thomas had stayed away from her for so long.

"I'm sorry," he continued, leaning against the railings beside her. "I wanted to come see you last night, tell you about the trek. It was a really good one. We went up to the waterfall..." He trailed off and fought back a yawn. "And this morning, well, I overslept and failed with the coffee delivery. I'm sorry."

Rose shrugged, trying to sound completely unfazed, as if it was no big deal and she'd barely noticed. "Don't apologise, it was an emergency."

"It made me think though, I should probably have your number. If I had it, I could have let you know."

Rose blinked twice. Had he just asked for her number?

Thomas was looking at her, expectantly, as if he was waiting for her to say something or do something.

"My number?"

"Your phone number."

"Right, of course!" Rose fumbled in her back pocket and scrolled to her contacts list. "I never remember my own number." Her cheeks were flushed and she could feel Thomas watching her as she read it out to him.

"Great," he said, plugging the number into his phone. "Now I can let you know if I'm going to miss a hot-drinks on the patio date."

Rose opened her mouth, but no sound came out. Now he'd called it a date?! She shimmied her shoulders, trying to shrug herself out of the daze she was in, but all she managed to say was, "Date?"

She expected Thomas to roll his eyes and laugh and say, *Well, not a date-date. Just a friendly date. You know, between friends.* But instead he said, "Yeah. Date." And, as he said it, she was certain that he moved a little closer.

Rose swallowed hard and looked away. "So," she said, steering the subject swiftly in a different direction. "Are you trekking again today?"

Thomas smiled at her, a knowing smile that said, *Okay, I won't push it,* and rested back on the railings, leaning on his elbows. "Not today. I called Chris and asked him to take over for most of the day. I'm too tired to be in control of guests *and* horses."

Rose laughed. "Fair enough. And you are the boss, you can give yourself the day off if you want to."

"Very good point," Thomas nodded. "So, I thought I'd

give myself the day off and see if you'd like to take a trip into the village with me? We need a few supplies and as wonderful as the ranch is, it seems a shame if you don't get to see anything else while you're here."

Instantly, Rose's entire body lightened. She had been certain that he was going to suggest they went to see the horses again, maybe even that she tried to ride one and, although she was feeling more confident and less terrified, she really wasn't sure she was ready for that kind of step.

"Sure," she said, beaming. "When do you want to leave?"

Thomas glanced at his watch. "An hour? I'll just make sure everyone knows what they're doing today, then we'll head off? It's not a short drive, but it's a nice one."

"As long as you drive a bit more carefully than the taxi driver who brought us here," Rose said warily, remembering how woozy she'd felt when she first arrived.

Thomas laughed. "I've lived here a long time, Rose. But I don't drive like an Italian *quite* yet."

As he walked away, Rose felt herself bob up and down on the balls of her feet. Yet again, she was failing miserably at making herself forget how stupidly handsome Thomas was. And he'd said the word 'date'.

Thomas had said 'date'.

This wasn't a good sign.

CHAPTER 12

"So, how did it even happen? You owning a ranch? I mean, you didn't ride when we were younger..." Sitting in the passenger seat of Thomas' truck, Rose trailed off, realising that for the first time in a long time she actually felt at ease. Not uncomfortable. Not awkward. Not worried she'd say the wrong thing. Just – easy.

"Katie didn't keep you informed over the years?"

Rose shrugged. "I guess not. Just in passing."

Thomas nibbled the corner of his lip, as if he wasn't sure whether he should be pleased that his sister hadn't gossiped about him or disappointed. "Well, obviously, I was kind of *different* when we first knew each other."

Rose tried to stifle a chuckle. She looked at Thomas from the corner of her eye but saw that he was smiling too. Back in school, he had been little more to Rose than

Katie's geeky older brother. He'd been overweight, spotty, and socially awkward.

"Just a bit?" she said, raising her eyebrows and trying not to look at the muscles in Thomas' broad shoulders or the way his beard somehow enhanced his jawline.

"The plan was that I was going to study maths, become an accountant–"

"Like me?"

"Yeah, except I'd have been a *terrible* accountant," Thomas laughed. "I took a year out before studying and decided that, for the first time in my life, I needed to be spontaneous. I was *sick* of being the guy who everyone thought of as boring and steady. So, I went to the airport and got on the first flight I could get a ticket for. I ended up in Rome. Met a guy who was going to spend a few weeks on a ranch mucking out horses, and decided to tag along."

"And that ranch was Heart of the Hills?"

"It was." Thomas left one hand on the steering wheel and rested the other casually in his lap. He shrugged. "And I guess I loved it so much I never left. The owner, Burt, he was this eccentric old American guy. He took a shine to me – said I had a natural way with the horses. So, he took me under his wing, taught me everything he knew, and when he died a few years back he left the whole place to me."

"Wow."

Thomas blinked slowly, as if it was no big deal. "He

had no kids. I guess after being here ten years, I'd become the closest thing to family that he had."

"So, it was yours – just like that?"

"Yep."

"You make it sound so easy. I don't think I could ever make a change like that. Do something so..." Rose looked out of the window, searching for the right word.

"Bonkers?'

"Brave!"

Thomas' eyes softened and he rubbed the back of his neck. He took his hat off and playfully balanced it on Rose's head. "Sure you could. Look at you. You're a lot braver than you think you are, Rose."

"I'm really not."

"Of course you are! The way you stepped in when Delilah was in trouble. The way you've started to face your fears. It's amazing. I'm in awe of you."

Rose began to blush. Katie's words resonated in her ears and she shook her head, as if the movement would dislodge her friend's voice from her brain.

Thomas was a smooth-talker. His own sister had told her so. And yet, when he said these things they seemed genuine. And they made Rose feel... invincible. But perhaps that's exactly what Katie had meant when she said Thomas was good at getting women to fall for him.

Rose consciously sat back a little in her seat and gave him back his hat. "So, where are we heading?"

Thomas drummed his fingers on the steering wheel. "Pettricci. It's pretty stunning."

"You said you need supplies?"

Thomas glanced at her. "I do. But also I wanted to take you out."

Rose swallowed hard. She didn't know how to respond, so chose not to. Instead, she leaned forward and turned on the radio. And they spent the rest of the journey singing along to a terrible 80's music station.

***

Pettricci was tiny. Up on a hillside with spectacular views over the countryside and a huge old villa at its centre, it was everything Rose had pictured and more.

As they wandered through the village square, Thomas stopped and bought fresh bread, olives and gelato from a small greengrocer's. Then, after walking for a while, he suggested they stop and eat.

Rose agreed, and as he magically pulled a picnic blanket from the backpack he'd surreptitiously slung over his shoulder when they left, she smiled to herself; it really did almost, just almost, feel like a date.

For once, because they were straying away from the ranch, she had chosen to change into a sundress. And when she sat down and stretched out her legs, she noticed Thomas looking at her.

"Everything okay?" she asked, feeling suddenly self-conscious.

"I was just thinking how nice you look." Thomas handed her a gelato and then grinned cheekily. "Dessert first, before it melts."

"I never say no to icecream," she replied, taking her tub from him while trying not to blush. Then, she wasn't sure where it came from, she heard herself saying, for the second time in the last few days, "So, do you do this with all of your guests? Take them out for picnics and gelato?"

She was watching him carefully, trying to decipher the way he'd react. But he simply tilted his head and said, very sincerely, "No. You're the first."

"Oh," she said. "Well, then I feel very lucky."

Thomas took his hat off and lay down on the picnic blanket, as if they had all the time in the world and he wasn't intending to go anywhere for the rest of the afternoon. "So do I, Rose. So do I."

They arrived back at the ranch just after supper. Somehow, accidentally, they had spent the entire day together. After their picnic lunch, they'd collected Thomas' supplies and then he'd purposefully taken a longer route home, stopping every now and then so that Rose could take photographs and marvel at the scenery.

"We missed dinner," she said, climbing out of the truck and looking around to see whether anyone had noticed them. For some reason, she felt like a teenager who'd disobeyed her parents' instructions. Like at any moment someone might jump out and say, "And where have you been, young lady?"

"Ah." Thomas raised his index finger and smiled. "No, we didn't. This way..." He waved towards the swimming pool then took Rose's hand and led her towards it.

She was just wondering how to wriggle out of a situation where Thomas would have to see her in her swimwear when they veered away from the pool, towards the enclosed Italian garden with its large pots and sparkling water fountain.

At the entrance, a space between two neatly manicured hedges, a red rope had been strung across the pathway and Rose stopped. "This wasn't here earlier."

"No, it wasn't." Thomas winked at her, lifted the rope and ushered her past.

When they emerged into the garden, arguably Rose's favourite spot on the entire ranch, she saw a table that wasn't usually there. And two chairs. And the smiling jolly chef who'd brought her and Katie their lunch on their first day.

Leaning closer, Thomas whispered, "I don't do this for all my guests either." And then he led her towards the table and pulled out a chair so that she could sit down.

The chef spoke quickly in Italian, grinning at the two

of them and waving at the food before leaving and re-tying the red rope behind her.

A little stunned, Rose shook her head and frowned. "Thomas, why did you do this?"

Thomas shrugged and looked down at his plate, nudging his food with his finger. "It's nice to have someone to do nice things for. That's all."

Rose didn't know what to say. If their trip to Pettricci had felt *almost* like a date, then this *definitely* felt like a date. And yet it wasn't. It couldn't be.

Trying to focus on her food, she diverted the conversation back to the ranch's smallholding and how Thomas had started it. She asked a million and one questions, all the time hoping that if she kept talking she'd eventually figure out how to say, *What is this, Thomas? Really?*

But she didn't. Eventually, she forgot that it was strange. And she forgot that Katie would be furious about it.

As Thomas laughed at her jokes and asked her about her life back home, she forgot that he was Thomas Goodwin – her best friend's brother – and she forgot that she absolutely was not the kind of girl who he'd usually date. And she felt, for the first time in a long time, content. Happy. Remarkable.

CHAPTER 13

"You know, you haven't asked me what's in store for tomorrow's 'Helping Rose Love Horses' lesson."

As they walked back towards her cabin, Rose breathed in deeply. A few days ago, she'd have been bubbling with nerves at the thought of spending time in close proximity to a horse. Now, though, it wasn't the horses that were making her nervous; it seemed like every time she tried to distance herself from Thomas, she failed. And after today, she didn't think she'd be able to resist whatever he suggested. "I'm flying home Tuesday, Thomas, are you sure there's any point?"

"Any point?" Thomas stopped dead in his tracks, as if he was utterly confused by what she'd said. "Of course there's a point! You're so close, Rose. All you need to do now is–" He widened his eyes and wiggled his eyebrows at her.

"Oh," she said, lifting her palms at him. "No, no. I don't think I can, Thomas. I managed to be close by without falling to bits but riding? It's–"

"Going to be an absolute breeze, trust me."

"I–"

Thomas made an *ah* sound and put his finger to her lips. "You can *do* this, Rose. You really can." He paused and took his finger away, letting it linger just below her ear, almost touching her neck.

He started walking again. His hand was close to hers, but he didn't reach for it.

"All right," she said, resolutely. "I'll think about it."

The next morning, Rose woke long before Thomas came knocking. She had agreed to try riding a horse. Why? Why had she said yes?

She wanted to back out. But, at the same time, she couldn't bear the idea of letting Thomas down; when she'd texted him before bed and said *Okay*, he'd seemed so excited. He'd said she could change her mind, and he meant it. She knew he meant it. But she didn't want to change her mind.

She wanted to do it. She wanted to conquer her fear and prove to herself, and him, and anyone who happened to be watching, that she wasn't the scared little goose that she appeared to be on the outside.

Unfortunately, her body didn't agree with her.

Even as she got out of bed, her legs were shaking. She felt physically sick and as if she might break out in a cold sweat at any moment.

Trying to ignore the clamour of sensations fighting to make her back out and stay in the cabin, she showered, dressed in jeans, sneakers, and a loose white top, then did a few star jumps in the middle of the room.

Years ago, when she'd been forced to deliver a series of presentations at work, she'd read a book about public speaking which said that fear triggers a 'fight or flight' response in the body. According to the book, if you can trick your body into thinking that you're fleeing, by moving about and raising your heart rate, then the nasty physical side effects of your fear will fade.

It hadn't worked back then – Rose had stuttered her way through five presentations before admitting defeat and asking Rebecca the intern to do it for her – and it wasn't working now.

She was simply more sweaty, and out of breath.

When Thomas tapped on the patio doors, Rose could barely force herself to open them. And as soon as he saw her, his eyes widened with concern. "Rose, you're as white as a ghost."

"I'm okay," she said, feeling green around the edges and like she might need to sit down before she fell down.

"Hey…" Thomas put his hands on her arms and smiled. "We don't have to do this today. I shouldn't have pushed you. Let's leave it until your next visit."

Trying to ignore the fact that Thomas had just mentioned a 'next visit', Rose shook her head. "No, I want to do it. I need to." She looked up and met his eyes, trying to conjure some kind of magic super-hero confidence from deep in her belly. "I'm sick of being scared of everything. So, I need to do something to help myself. Like you did. When you came here."

Thomas breathed in slowly. She couldn't tell what he was thinking, but he was studying her face with a softness in his eyes that she hadn't seen before. "Okay then," he said. "Let's do it."

They had agreed to head out early, to avoid bumping into any other guests. But the stables were still buzzing with activity – stalls being mucked out, horses being exercised around the smaller paddocks, saddles and reins being prepared for the day's treks.

Rose stopped and took a deep breath. She was trembling.

Thomas put his arm around her and squeezed. "One step at a time, okay?"

She nodded, unable to speak.

"See that empty paddock there?"

Rose nodded again.

"Go down there and wait under the trees. I'll fetch Massimo. He's an absolute sweetheart. Small, gentle... you'll love him when you meet him. I promise."

Rose tried to speak but all that came out was a whisper. "Okay."

When she reached the paddock, away from the stables and from other people, she felt a tiny bit better.

Waiting for Thomas, she tried to remember how she'd felt when she looked into Delilah's eyes, when she'd stroked Piccolo and given him his name, and when she'd watched Thomas going off on his trek.

He was completely at ease around the horses, as were pretty much all of the other riders, instructors and stable hands. Not once had she seen a horse kick up on its hind legs, bolt off into the blue with a rider shouting for help, or any of the other things she'd imagined happening when she'd seen horses in the past.

You can do this, Rose, she whispered to herself.

And then, she saw Thomas. He emerged from the yard, leading a small sandy brown horse with a blonde mane.

Thomas was taller than the horse and was smiling and chatting to it as they approached. Slowly, taking in Rose's almost translucent complexion, he led Massimo up beside her and stopped a few feet away.

Rose smiled, trying desperately to make her body play

ball and calm itself down. "He looks friendly," she said shakily.

"He is. Aren't you, boy?" Thomas stroked Massimo's nose and the horse nuzzled into him.

Rose stepped forward.

"Always approach them from the front, so you don't surprise them. That's the only real thing you have to worry about." Thomas moved towards Rose and took her hand. Entwining his fingers with hers, he lifted her hand and stretched it out so that her fingertips brushed ever-so-gently against the horse's mane.

Rose was holding her breath. She expected Massimo to whinny or shake his head. But he didn't. In fact, he almost leaned into her touch.

With his hand on top of hers, Thomas guided her fingers down to Massimo's nose. It was soft and smoother than she'd expected. And when Thomas took his hand away, she let hers stay where it was, gently moving up and down until the queasy feeling in her stomach started to subside.

"We use Massimo a lot when we do therapy with local kids," Thomas said softly. "He's a real star and he's *very* intuitive. It's like he knows exactly what you're feeling. When someone's more confident, he becomes playful and a bit silly. But when they're nervous, he's as still as anything. A picture of calm and tranquillity." Thomas patted Massimo's shoulder. "Aren't you, boy?"

Rose was transfixed. Doing what Thomas said and

taking one step at a time was working. All she was thinking about was stroking Massimo's mane and nose and shoulder. She wasn't thinking about what came next.

"We can do this for as long as you like, there's no rush," Thomas said, stepping back to give her some space.

Rose nodded. "I think I'm ready," she said, quickly, because if she didn't then she might not say it at all.

"Really?" Thomas took off his hat and rested it on a nearby fence post. "Take more time, Rose, if you need it."

"No." She shook her head. "I think I need to do it now, before I have the chance to get nervous again."

"All right." Thomas gestured to a small wooden stump by the fence. "You can use this to help you up." He patted Massimo and moved him over towards the stump, then took Rose's arm and helped her up onto it. It was barely a foot off the ground, but her legs were wobbling so much she felt like she was standing on top of the Empire State Building.

Patting the stirrup closest to them, Thomas told her to put her left foot into it, hold on to the front of the saddle, and then just swing her right leg over. "Don't be afraid that you'll hurt him. You won't. Use the saddle to help yourself up. Okay?"

Rose's throat was constricting. Her mouth was dry and she suddenly desperately wished she'd brought a flask of water with her. Nodding, she took a long deep breath, lifted up her foot and placed it into the stirrup. Remembering how the other riders had done it, she closed her eyes, counted to three, opened them, reached up and grabbed Massimo's saddle and then – just like that – she was up.

She was sitting in the saddle.

"Ha!" She let out a half-gasp half-shout. "I did it!" Turning to Thomas, she grinned at him. "I did it!"

Thomas was smiling proudly. "You're a natural," he said, nodding at her as if he really was impressed.

Rose reached out her hands and stroked Massimo's mane. He hadn't even moved. He had just stood quietly and allowed her to heave herself up onto his back. And now that she was there looking down at the ground, instead of feeling wobbly and unsteady, she felt strong. She felt secure.

At least, she did until Thomas clapped his hands and said, "Right, are you ready for a walk around the paddock?"

CHAPTER 14

*R*eturning to the ranch house, Rose was almost giddy with pride.

She'd spent nearly an hour riding up and down the paddock, then helped Thomas take off Massimo's saddle and reins, groomed him and led him back into the stable.

She still felt a little jumpy when he moved unexpectedly, or when other horses came a bit too close. But on the whole, she felt like an entirely different person from the one who'd almost backed out and stayed home that morning.

Thomas seemed pretty happy too and had spent most of the day complimenting her – telling her she was a natural rider, so much more confident than he'd imagined she'd be, so self-assured in the saddle.

When they reached the terrace, Thomas disappeared

inside to fetch them some drinks and Rose sat smiling to herself.

Picturing an evening of dinner and laughter and heart-to-heart talks, she was wondering whether she should go back to the cabin and change when Thomas appeared beside her. Except, this time he wasn't alone.

"I was just telling everyone how fantastic you were," he said, grinning. Behind him, Fleur smiled at her while Chris and Mike nodded approvingly. "Sit down, guys." Thomas gestured to the seats around the table.

"Amazing progress you've made, Rose. In such a short time." Fleur sat down beside Thomas and flicked her hair over her shoulder. For some reason, whenever Fleur spoke, Rose felt as if she was scrutinising her in some way.

"Well, it was all thanks to Thomas," she said, trying not to allow the usual notes of awe and wonder to grace her voice when she looked at him.

"I told you he's good at this kind of thing." Fleur's hand rested on Thomas' forearm and it made Rose blink uncomfortably. Thomas, however, didn't even seem to notice. He just poured himself a drink, sat back, and laced his fingers together behind his head, jutting out his elbows as if he'd never been so relaxed.

"How long are you here for, Rose?" Chris smiled at her politely as he passed her a tumbler full of iced tea.

"Not much longer. I fly home Tuesday."

"Shame," he replied. "Now you're getting into your

stride. Still, I'm sure Tom will invite you back." Chris gave Thomas a knowing look and Thomas narrowed his eyes slightly.

Rose had the uneasy sensation that she was missing something – an inference she didn't quite understand or an inside joke. She smiled, then glanced at Thomas.

"You can visit whenever you like," he said, sincerely.

Beside her, Chris coughed and she was certain that he was hiding a smirk behind his hand.

Interrupting them, however, Fleur leaned forward and put both palms firmly on the table in front of her. "Who's up for a game of poker tonight? It's been ages and I feel like kicking some butt."

Mike rolled his eyes. "Nah, not again."

"Oh come on," she said with a pout. "Rossi's up for it. I called him earlier."

"Rossi's always up for a card game. And he pretty much always wins," Chris added. "But, yeah, sure. I'm in. Tom?"

Thomas sipped his drink and glanced sideways at Rose, then nodded at them. "Sure. Why not? Although you do know it's bad form to beat your boss at cards, right?"

The other three laughed, and when they stopped, Rose realised they were all looking at her. Fleur tilted her head in a movement that reminded Rose of a small delicate bird. "Rose?"

"Me?"

"Sure. You game?"

Rose swallowed hard. But then she surprised herself by saying, "Okay. I'm in."

After dinner, Rose returned to her cabin to collect her long sleeved black sweater and a scarf. As soon as the sun went down, it became chilly and she wasn't good in the cold.

Fleur's poker game was due to start as soon as the guests had made their way back to their cabins after dinner. Rose wasn't really a fan of late nights. But, not that she'd let on to the others, she *was* a fan of poker.

And, more than that, she was good at it.

It was probably the one secret talent that she had. The one thing that had ever impressed people. Because they just didn't expect it of her.

Fleur and Mike had made quite a big deal of the fact that Rossi the vet was a phenomenal poker player, but Rose was quietly confident that she could take him on. *If* she kept her skills under wraps for as long as possible.

When she returned to the ranch house, Thomas had moved tables and chairs aside, lit the giant fire pit in the centre of the terrace, and set up a poker table beside it.

Fleur was already seated and was staring at Rossi, who was opposite her, with a steely look in her eyes.

For a moment, Rose lingered by the steps, but then she remembered how good she'd felt when she'd ridden up and down the paddock that morning, so she took a deep breath and walked casually towards the group.

As soon as she sat down, beside Rossi, Fleur introduced them. He seemed friendly and Rose had to admit, although considerably older than the rest of them, he was pretty good looking; very *Italian*. Dark hair, a neat beard flecked with grey, and eyes that twinkled when he spoke.

He kissed her hand as he said hello.

"Hi, nice to meet you."

"You're the brave lady who helped Delilah in her hour of need?" Rossi asked, smiling and still not letting go of Rose's hand.

"I am," she said, taking it back and sliding it slightly awkwardly into her lap.

Rossi smiled and nodded smoothly at her. "And have you played poker before, Rose?"

"Oh," she shrugged. "A little. Not since college though, really."

Rossi nodded, not even attempting to hide his smile.

"You shouldn't have told him that, Rose," Fleur said, leaning across the table towards them. "He'll use it to his advantage."

Rose blinked at Fleur, as if she didn't really know what she meant, and Fleur giggled. "You'll see."

After a few more minutes of chit chat and pouring drinks, they were ready to start.

Thomas had chosen to sit beside Fleur, so Rose was sandwiched between Rossi and Mike.

"Maybe we should do a practise run first, for Rose," Fleur said, kindly.

"Oh no, that's okay, I'm sure I'll get the hang of it." Rose was already looking at her hand. It was a good one and she didn't particularly want to waste it on a fake round.

"No, that's a good idea. Refresh your memory," Thomas said, smiling.

"Okay, if you're sure?" Rose bit back her annoyance and started to squint at her cards. Beside her, Rossi leaned closer and said, "Shall I take a look, help you figure it out?"

Rose blinked at him. She wasn't keen on the fact he was so close to her but she ignored it and nodded, laughing a little. "Yes, please. I've no idea what this means."

When she showed him her hand, Rossi laughed, slapped his thigh and looked around at the rest of the table. "Good job this is a practise round, she'd have thrashed us all with this."

"Would I?" said Rose, wondering if she was overdoing her naivity. But when no one seemed to question it, she carried on, nodding and saying *ohhh* as Rossi explained that she was holding what they called a 'Full House'.

"Okay," she said, after listening to the rules three times and playing along with the 'fake' round. "I think I've got it."

"Well," said Mike kindly. "It takes a while to get to

really understand it all but just keep your bets low and enjoy it, yeah?"

Rose smiled at him. "Good idea. Thank you."

An hour later, Rose and Rossi were the only two players left in the game. Fleur and Mike were convinced that Rose was simply experiencing beginners luck, but Chris and Thomas were watching her intently and she was almost certain that Thomas had figured her out.

Rossi, on the other hand, was so self-assured that she knew he wouldn't even contemplate folding.

"I'll raise you," Rose said, confidently.

Rossi's eyebrows twitched. "Are you sure? I shouldn't really do this, Rose, but I'm giving you an out here."

"I'm sure," she said, pushing forwards her little stack of money.

Rossi smirked, matched her bid, then slowly exposed his cards. "Four of a kind," he said, looking around the table as if he was expecting a round of applause.

He was reaching forwards, ready to take his winnings, when Rose said, "Hang on," and spread her cards out in front of her.

Around her, the others gasped and *ooooh*'d.

"I'm not quite sure, but I *think* this is called a 'Straight Flush'?" She furrowed her brow quizzically, then allowed her lips to spread into a wide and dazzling grin.

"Ha!" shouted Thomas. "Rossi, she got you!"

Rossi sat back in his chair, as if he was full of air and someone had just deflated him. "This whole thing," he said, waving his hand at her. "It was an act?"

Rose shrugged, gathering her money and taking a sip of her drink. "Maybe," she said, coyly. "Maybe not."

When she looked up, while the others were thumping Rossi on the back and telling him he'd have better luck next time, Thomas was watching her. He blinked quickly when she met his eyes and looked away. But then he got up from the table and walked over to where she was sitting. "Shall I walk you back?" he asked, glancing towards the cabins.

"Sure." Rose stifled a yawn. "It is *way* past my bedtime and winning really does take it out of you, you know."

"Night Rose," Mike and Chris called. But as Rose looked back, she noticed that Fleur was watching them. And she didn't look happy.

Interrupting her train of thought, Thomas slung his arm around her shoulders and said, "That was incredible. I knew you were faking it – the whole 'I don't know what I'm doing' thing. I just knew it."

"Is that why you folded so early?" Rose asked, trying to keep her brain from doing somersaults because she was tucked neatly under Thomas' arm and so close to him that she could smell his sweet, dusky cologne.

"You bet," he laughed. "And you have no idea how good it was to see Rossi get taken down a peg or two."

Rose shuddered as she remembered how close he'd gotten to her. "Mmm. He's quite full on."

"Certainly is," Thomas nodded.

As they reached her cabin, they paused just in front of the little flint wall. "Thomas," she said, quietly.

"Mmm." Was he moving a little closer?

"Thank you for today. It was..."

"It was pretty great, huh?"

"It was."

"*You* were great." Thomas was definitely closer to her than he had been a moment ago. His grey T-shirt emphasised the sun-drenched complexion of his skin, and beneath his neat beard, Rose was certain that his cheeks were dimpling as he smiled at her. "Remarkable Rose."

His hand was beside hers, lingering there, almost touching. And just when she thought he might wind his fingers around hers, a voice behind them shouted, "Thomas?! You up for round two? Rossi wants to win back his losses."

Thomas turned and looked over his shoulder. Fleur was standing a little way away, waving. "I–"

"It's okay," Rose said, stepping back and starting to fumble for her key in her jeans pocket. "I'm tired. But you go. Have fun. I'll see you tomorrow."

Thomas smiled, although it wasn't the smile she was used to seeing.

"Thomas!" Fleur called, motioning for him to hurry up.

"Okay," he shouted back. Then he leaned forward, kissed Rose swiftly on the cheek, and jogged back to the ranch house.

CHAPTER 15

The following day, Thomas brought coffee, as always, and they sat drinking it and watching the sun come up, as always.

But, for some reason, deep in her stomach Rose now felt... reticent.

Something about the way Fleur had looked at her last night and the way she'd called Thomas back to the group had butted up against what Katie had said – that Thomas had a different girlfriend every week – and left Rose wondering if she'd been completely misguided. Could Thomas be using her to make Fleur jealous? Or was he simply the kind of guy who was nice to everyone, who made *all* women feel like they were supermodels because of the way he looked at them with his deep, smouldering, chocolate brown eyes.

Had their date in the Italian gardens simply been a kind gesture? A *friendly* gesture?

Sighing, she finished her coffee and set it down on the ground.

"You okay?" Thomas asked. "I thought after your triumph last night, you'd be on top of the world."

"I'm fine, good, just tired."

"Well, maybe you should spend today relaxing," he said, getting up and scooping her empty flask into his hand. "I'm leading a beginners' trek this morning and have a stack of paperwork to do this afternoon. So I may have to abandon you for a while."

"That's fine," said Rose, almost relieved. "I could do with some time to come down from my winner's high." She tried to smile, but she knew it didn't quite reach her eyes because Thomas frowned.

"Okay, if you're sure you're all right?"

"I'm sure," she said, waving him off. "See you later. If you're about."

For most of the day, however, Thomas was not about. He flitted past every now and then but, largely, was too busy to stop and chat.

Rose both missed him and was relieved to have some distance from him at the same time. The way he made her feel when he sauntered up to her was beginning to become impossible to ignore. The almost-touches and the smiles and the kind words were too much.

And she'd been giving in to them. She'd been so close to letting herself kiss him. But then something had planted a horrible niggling seed of doubt in her brain that she couldn't seem to dislodge.

It was the way Fleur had behaved last night, and the things Katie had said. Together, they were toxic. And it was making Rose's head hurt.

So, after spending the main part of the afternoon by the pool, she retreated to the cabin and read her book on the patio.

It was almost dinner time and her stomach was rumbling when Fleur walked by.

Rose stood up and waved before she could stop herself.

"Rose, hey." Fleur walked over and leaned on the wall, the way Thomas did. "You were awesome last night. Well done."

Now, without Thomas around, Fleur was being completely normal. Or, perhaps she'd always been completely normal and Rose had simply imagined the strange looks and brusque behaviour. "Thanks," she said. "How was the second game?"

"Good. Rossi won. Obviously."

"Obviously," Rose replied. She wanted to ask about Thomas. But she didn't know how and suddenly, horribly awkwardly, she found herself saying, "So, Fleur, you and

Thomas seem pretty close..." She trailed off, feeling her cheeks start to flush.

For a moment, Fleur simply looked at her. But then she laughed. "Yeah, I guess we are. Why'd you ask?"

"Oh, nothing really. Katie made some comment about him having lots of girlfriends but he's seemed pretty well behaved since I've been here."

Fleur laughed. "Okay. Well, firstly, Thomas doesn't do *girlfriends*. He does fun. Easy, laid back, nothing serious. You know – no big deal kind of thing."

"And secondly?"

"Secondly, he's bound to be on his best behaviour around you. He doesn't want you reporting back to his sister!"

Rose tried to laugh.

"Listen, I've got to go. I won't tell Thomas that you're spying on him for his little sister though, okay?"

Rose smiled, as if it was all a funny joke. "Thanks," she said, waving.

As Fleur walked away, Rose watched her. She watched her easy movements and confident stride, her long legs and her TV commercial hair. And when she looked down at her own mis-matched outfit, pale skin, and thick calves, she sighed.

When she was around Thomas, she felt as if he saw her, and liked her. She felt the hum of attraction between them. A vibration that hung in the air whenever they were close.

Surely, Thomas wasn't that good an actor? But then maybe he just couldn't help it. Maybe that was how he was with *all* females. And Rose was doing precisely what Katie had warned her not to – reading too much into it and getting too involved.

Sighing, she sat back down and put her head in her hands.

It had been a long time since she'd felt this way about a guy. Usually, she kept her guard up and a good amount of distance between herself and anyone who could possibly cause her to experience hurt or embarrassment.

But maybe that was it; maybe, deep down in her subconscious, her brain thought that Thomas was a safe bet because she'd be leaving in a few days and she'd never have to see him again. So, her silly, messed up self had allowed all these feelings to happen just for the thrill of feeling them. Because there was absolutely no way they'd turn into anything more than a crush. Because there was no way he'd reciprocate them.

Feeling a little better, Rose nodded to herself; that had to be it. This whole thing was just a harmless bit of fun. A schoolgirl flutter that was lovely to feel and would be left behind the second she got on the plane home.

Why not let Thomas make her feel special? Why not allow him to smile at her and be nice to her? As long as she knew it wouldn't lead anywhere, what was the harm in it?

Harmless fun. That's what it was – harmless fun.

CHAPTER 16

*L*ater that night, after squirrelling away a giant takeaway box of salad to eat in her room, Rose was texting Katie to tell her about her poker triumph when, for the first time in at least six hours, she saw Thomas in the distance.

Usually, he walked towards her with a great big grin on his face but this evening she couldn't see his smile; he walked slowly, as if he was preoccupied, and by the time he got to her Rose was certain that something was the matter.

Putting down her phone, she climbed over the wall and walked to meet him.

"Are you all right? Is it Delilah again?"

Thomas narrowed his eyes for a second, then shook his head. "No, no, she's fine." He sighed and took up his usual stance on the wall. "It's not Delilah."

Rose perched beside him. She wanted to reach out and touch his hand; he looked worried and it was an expression she wasn't used to seeing on his face. Pretty much every time they'd talked since she'd arrived at the ranch, Thomas had been full of light and energy – a trait he shared with Katie.

"What is it?" Rose ducked her head to meet his eyes. "This morning you were full of the joys of spring."

Thomas took a deep breath and then let it all out in a great big whoosh of air. "It's the volunteers."

"Volunteers?" Rose looped back through her memory, trying to recall what he'd told her about them.

"We're supposed to have a group of ten arriving at the end of the week, to help out over the summer."

Usually, Thomas was completely at ease with making conversation but suddenly Rose felt as if she was having to drag it out of him. "So, there's a problem with their arrival?"

Thomas brushed his fingers through his thick dark hair. "We arrange it all through a company in the U.K. They book the volunteers' flights, ensure they're good candidates and that we keep up our end of the deal – you wouldn't believe the amount of places that *promise* good food and accommodation and then try to get away with putting their volunteers in nothing better than a shed for the summer."

Rose nodded; she definitely *would* believe it.

"Well, I was informed this afternoon that the company

has gone into administration. All the trips they organised have been grounded. No one seems to know what's going on but I'm pretty sure no one will be arriving on Friday. The agency said that they would pass on my details to everyone who booked, to see if they want to try and make it here under their own steam, but I can't imagine they will. I mean, they don't even know if they'll get their money back."

"That's awful, Thomas. I'm so sorry."

Thomas shrugged and offered her a resigned smile. "So, it looks like we're going to be short staffed over our busiest time of year. I spoke to Fleur, she can stick around. She was supposed to be heading off fruit picking or something but she's pretty flexible, comes and goes as she pleases really."

Rose tried to ignore the softening of his smile and the ever-so-slight widening of his eyes as he said Fleur's name. "Can any of the others stay?"

"Not really. Most have other jobs to move on to."

"Gosh, Thomas, I'm sorry. I don't know what to suggest."

Thomas laughed. "Me neither! We've got enough instructors. That's not a problem. But we rely on volunteers over the summer to get all the grunt work done. I could reach out to the local villages, but they're not really interested. That's why we started the scheme in the first place."

Rose opened her mouth to speak, but stopped herself.

What she was about to say was *crazy*. A few hours ago, she'd sat in this very spot and come to terms with the fact that it was okay for her to have a giant crush on Thomas because she'd be leaving in a couple of days' time. But then, despite the voice in her head that was screaming, *Don't say it!* she said it anyway. "If I stuck around, could I help?

She winced slightly as she waited for Thomas' reply; surely, he would say, *Don't be so ridiculous Rose. What help could you possibly be?* But he was silent. For a moment, he didn't look at her, just looked straight ahead and drummed his fingers on his thigh. Then he turned to her. "Really? You'd do that?"

Rose shrugged, as if it was no big deal. As if her stomach wasn't twisting into somersault shapes at the idea of staying a bit longer, and having a few more conversations with him, and seeing him striding towards her with coffee as the sun came up over the horizon each morning.

"What about work?"

Rose swallowed hard but tried to sound confident as she replied, "I'm owed a lot of vacation time. And I can help them out by email. I'm sure it would be fine."

In reality, she had absolutely no idea if it would be fine. It was true that she hadn't taken much vacation time last year, or the year before. But, still, it was very, very unusual to ring and ask for another three weeks off in the middle of a vacation. Her boss liked her, but she was pretty sure he didn't like her *that* much.

"Rose, I don't really know what to say. You *hated* horses two weeks ago."

Rose looked towards the fields in the distance and tried to make her tense shoulders relax. She definitely felt more comfortable with them now. But was she really up to diving in and helping take care of them? "I guess you helped me change my mind about them," she said, looking down at her hands. "I'm not saying that I would be very much help but if you want me to stay, and if my boss says yes..."

Thomas' lips spread into a huge grin that made his cheeks dimple beneath his beard. "Rose!" He reached forward, pulling her into an embrace and planting a succession of light butterfly kisses on her cheek. "You're amazing. Thank you."

Rose's heart fluttered and she tried to calm it down. Thomas had caught her eyes with his and wasn't letting go. His hands were on her upper arms and he was smiling at her. But it was a softer smile. A smile that said he might brush her hair from her face and lean in towards her. A dangerous smile.

She swallowed hard and swung her legs over the wall to land back on her side of it. Then she clapped her hands. "Right, well, I'll email them now then. Work... I'll email work."

Thomas stood up too, on the other side. "Sure. Great. Thank you, Rose. And while you do that, I'll go see if I can persuade Mike and Chris to stick around.

With you guys and Fleur we might *just* be able to manage."

Rose waved goodbye and ducked back into her cabin. Sitting down on the bed, she pulled her laptop from her suitcase and fired it up.

Although a huge part of her wanted to stay, a bigger part was suddenly hoping that her boss would say no; if he said no, she could go home and forget all about Thomas. She could get on with her life and never, ever have to face the fact that she was developing an absolutely enormous crush on him. A crush he would never reciprocate and which, even if he did, couldn't possibly lead anywhere because he was her best friend's brother.

Briefly, she wondered whether she should simply tell Thomas that her boss had said no. But if Thomas asked to see his reply, and discovered she'd never emailed in the first place, he'd think she was awful.

So, quickly, because then she wouldn't have the chance to change her mind, she wrote:

Dear Craig,

I hope all is going well back at the office.

Italy is lovely, but I'm emailing with a slightly unusual request.

As you know, I'm staying with a family friend and he's run into some difficulty. It would help immensely if I could stay on for a few weeks.

I believe I carried over ten days' vacation time last year, and the same the year before. So, I was hoping I might be able to use them now and return to work at the end of August.

I have my laptop with me, so I could address anything urgent via email and I'd be happy to video call regularly too if it would help.

I completely understand if this isn't possible.

Thank you and best wishes,

Rose.

Pressing send, Rose held her breath. She and Craig had quite a casual boss-employee relationship. He was a bit of a maverick in terms of his management style, always preferring to trust that his workers had done their allotted hours rather than keep track of their movements.

If an employee wanted to arrive at ten and work until six thirty, he just assumed they would keep their word and let them get on with it. He had even once given the entire department permission to go and see a movie in the middle of the day because they couldn't get tickets for the evening showing.

But an extra *twenty* days off was a big deal.

Rose closed her laptop and sighed. Then she buried herself under the covers and tried to thinking of something – anything – that wasn't Thomas Goodwin.

CHAPTER 17

*C*raig replied to Rose's email at three a.m. The ping from her phone woke her up and, as soon as she saw his name, her heart almost leapt into her throat.

She had absolutely no idea whether she was hoping he'd said yes or no to her request and staring at the bright light of her phone screen was making her eyes blurry.

Squinting at it, she tried to decipher the words in the email.

Dear Rose,

I'm glad you're having a great time on vacation. Usually, we wouldn't approve such a request. HOWEVER, you have been an exceptional employee for many years. I looked at your personnel file and can see that you've never used up all of your annual leave and have had only two sick days in the entire time you've worked here.

So, I think you deserve some good will from us in return.

I can't stretch to three weeks, as this is reserved for our honeymooners, but if you can agree to two hour-long video chats each week and to be available on email for urgent enquiries, then I will grant permission for you to remain for another fourteen days.

Let me know your decision,

Craig

Rose read the email at least ten times before replying to say thank you and yes and thank you again. Then she turned her phone off and lay staring at the ceiling, trying to decide how to tell Katie that she wouldn't be returning home in two days' time.

Surely, Katie would know the reason. Surely, she'd guess that Rose was staying to help Thomas because she was becoming ever so slightly infatuated with him.

At five a.m., Rose gave up trying to get back to sleep and got up.

She was sitting on the patio, huddled beneath a blanket and watching the sun begin to rise, when she finally took out her phone and texted Thomas.

My boss said yes, he gave me another two weeks. So, it looks like you've got a new stable hand.

Then, she took a deep breath, and texted Katie.

Weird news – Thomas' volunteers aren't coming. The agency he used is in trouble so all trips have been cancelled.

I said I'd stay and help out for another fortnight. Not sure what help I'll be but it seems like it's all hands on deck.

As she pressed 'send' a heavy, anxious, twitching sensation settled in her chest. She wasn't lying to Katie. But by omitting to tell her about her feelings for Thomas, she was – for the first time since they were teenagers – allowing an imaginary wedge to form between them. She didn't like it. But, at the same time, she didn't know how to stop it.

She couldn't seem to prevent her feelings for Thomas. Like a rolling stone gathering moss, they simply grew and grew and grew every time she saw him or spoke to him.

Reeling back through her memory, she tried to figure out whether there was a time when she could have stopped it happening. But right from the second she saw him, she'd been captivated.

Maybe if Katie hadn't gone home. Or if Rose had gone back with her, it would have all just fizzled away and come to nothing.

But spending time together, alone, as if they were just two people who'd met and hit it off, had added infinite fuel to the fire. And now Rose had no idea how to put it out.

The only thing she could think of was to tell Thomas how she felt. Because she was pretty sure that if she did that – if she told him she was thinking about him all day every day, and that he turned her legs to jelly, and that all she wanted was to be close to him – he'd almost definitely tell her, very politely, that he just didn't see her that way.

He'd tell her that he liked her as a friend, and that they'd had a great time together, and that he would hate to hurt her feelings but that all he could offer her was friendship.

And, yes, she'd be embarrassed and want the ground to swallow her up. But at least maybe then they really could be friends; she could spend the next fourteen days simply enjoying her newfound confidence and helping out her *friend* without thinking about how tantalising his lips were every time he smiled at her.

By the time Thomas arrived with her coffee, at six thirty on the dot, Rose had made up her mind. Just as she'd done when she conquered her fear of riding and climbed up into the saddle, she would bite back her nerves and tell Thomas that she liked him.

And then all the guilt and the anxious anticipation would disappear.

"Got your text. Amazing news." Thomas hopped over the wall in one swift movement and planted himself firmly in the chair beside her. "Rose, you've got no idea how grateful I am."

"Well," she said, already finding it hard to speak. "I'm not sure how much help I'll be."

Thomas rolled his eyes. "Come on, you'll be great. You know you will."

Rose breathed in slowly, sucking air past her front teeth and tapping her fingers on her flask of coffee.

"You okay? Did your boss give you a hard time? Because if he did—"

"No, no, Craig was great. Very accommodating."

"Okaay..." Thomas ducked his head to try and scrutinise her face. "Then..."

Rose looked up at him, then swiftly returned her gaze to her coffee. Closing her eyes and biting her lower lip, she braced herself for what she was about to say. "Thomas, there's something I think I need to say to you..."

She daren't look up, and Thomas didn't say anything.

"I like you." She said it quickly, too quickly, sputtering it out in the most ineloquent way imaginable.

"I like you too," Thomas replied, cheerfully.

Rose sighed, then forced herself to look at him. "No, I mean, I *like* you. A lot. A distracting amount, actually. And I'm telling you because I feel awful about it. Katie would hate it. She told me explicitly to stay away from you but I've done the exact opposite. And I know you don't feel the same. I know that. Because, well, why would you? So, I guess that's why I'm telling you. Because if I hear you say it – say that we're just friends – then maybe I'll be able to forget about it and go back to being normal and—"

Thomas had been watching her carefully but suddenly waved his hands at her. "Woah. Rose. Stop."

Almost out of breath from talking so fast, she swallowed hard and felt herself wince.

"I'm so sorry," he said softly.

Rose gripped the side of her chair with one hand and her coffee cup with the other.

Thomas leaned in, lowering his voice to a whisper. "I'm sorry because I think I'm going to upset my sister."

Rose frowned at him. He was smiling.

He shook his head, laughing as he reached out for her hand. "I like you too."

Rose's mouth almost fell open.

"I mean, I *like* you. A lot."

Inside, a voice in Rose's head was screaming, *No, no, no, no! This isn't how it was supposed to go! He's supposed to say you're just friends!* But her heart was dancing a jig. "You *like* me?"

Thomas laughed, louder this time, then slowly took the flask from her and set it on the floor. Leaning in, he put both hands on her thighs. His touch was light and warm and sent a wave of butterflies from her stomach all the way up to her cheeks. She was grinning, but she couldn't help it.

"I like you," he said, softly. And then he kissed her.

Thomas Goodwin kissed her.

His beard bristled against her chin as his lips touched hers. She moved her hands up to his shoulders and wrapped her arms around his neck. And then suddenly he was picking her up and twirling her round. And when he set her down again, everything was different.

CHAPTER 18

ELEVEN DAYS LATER

"Rose? Is Massimo ready?" Chris was carrying two saddles at once and dashing across the stable yard. Two treks were due to leave the ranch that morning and they were struggling to get the horses out and lined up.

"He certainly is." Rose patted Massimo's nose as she led him towards the gate.

"Great, thank you."

"I can do Stella's saddle if you like?" Rose tethered Massimo to his post then took the second saddle from Chris.

"Really?" Chris narrowed his eyes at her; Stella was *huge*. One of the biggest horses on the ranch, she had big heavy hooves, thick legs and a large behind which always made Rose smile.

"Yeah, it's okay. I'm okay." Rose walked slowly towards Stella. After agreeing to stay on, there had been very little time for her to remain nervous. Instantaneously, she'd immersed herself in the workings of the ranch and, to her utter disbelief, she'd enjoyed every second of it.

Largely, she'd stuck with the smaller, gentler horses. Thomas had allocated her three to look after, plus Piccolo the foal, and he'd shown her how to groom them, exercise them and prepare their saddles. She'd been doing a pretty good job. But she hadn't ventured too close to the larger ones. She had her little group, who she knew and trusted, and had so far stuck to them like glue.

But, now, approaching Stella, she actually felt... okay. More than okay – confident.

She'd just finished fastening the saddle and was splashing her face with water from the tap by the barn, because the temperature in the last week had sky-rocketed, when she spotted Thomas and a crowd of recently-arrived riders walking down from the ranch house.

Thomas was at the front of the group, chatting casually to a woman with long dark hair. She was smiling and laughing loudly at his jokes. A few weeks ago, watching them would have given Rose a horrible sinking feeling in the pit of her stomach.

It still niggled a little, in the back of her mind somewhere, but she ignored it. Every day since Thomas kissed her, she had chosen to ignore it. Maybe if he'd been secretive about it, she'd have remained wary. Maybe if he'd told her they should act 'normal' around the others, she'd have thought he was trying to hide something. But, far from secretive, he was the opposite.

The first time he put his arm around her in front of Fleur and Mike, Rose had almost jumped out of her skin. But then he'd casually squeezed her into him and kissed her on the forehead and Rose had grinned like the Cheshire Cat.

Fleur had looked surprised but had remained silent and, ever since, Rose had seen very little of her.

So, as they approached, Rose straightened her shoulders, held her head up high, and walked over to the group knowing that Thomas would greet her with a kiss.

Of course, he did. And the brunette beside him immediately stopped fluttering her eyelashes and smiled, almost apologetically, at Rose.

"Everything okay?" Thomas asked her, tucking her hair behind her ear.

"Good," she said, knowing she was flushed from the heat but, for once, not feeling self-conscious about it.

Thomas waved the group towards Mike and Chris, who divided them into two – beginners and advanced – and began allocating them their horses.

"Where are you headed today?" Rose asked, absent-mindedly stroking Thomas' arm.

"Up to the hills, it'll be a long one. Sorry."

"That's okay," she replied. "Plenty here to keep me busy."

"Rose, you've been working *way* too hard."

"Got to earn my keep – you *are* letting me stay in one of the best cabins totally free of charge."

"As if I'd make my girlfriend stay anywhere else?"

Thomas kept walking, towards the group of riders who were now waiting patiently to begin their trek, but Rose had stopped in her tracks. Girlfriend?

She should ask him. She should say it, right there: *Thomas, did you just call me your girlfriend?* But she didn't. She couldn't. Instead, she just jogged up to him, stood beside Stella as Thomas swung himself effortlessly into her saddle, and then waved him goodbye.

At lunch time, she joined Chris, Fleur, and the small group of other instructors and stable hands that Thomas had managed to gather together when the volunteers failed to arrive.

Now, she sat at the cool kids' table. And it *almost* felt normal.

"So..." Allison, one of the instructors who'd arrived at the last minute, on loan from a friend of Thomas' at a nearby ranch, smiled at her with wide, interested eyes. "You and Thomas – are you?" She leaned in towards Rose conspiratorially, as if they were high school friends gossiping about boys.

"Oh, we're..." Rose trailed off, then laughed. "I'm not really sure what we are."

"Well you *look* super cute together," Allison grinned. American with an open, friendly face and freckles on the bridge of her nose, Rose had immediately been drawn to her. In a way, she reminded Rose of Katie, which brought back the uneasy feeling in her stomach.

As Allison went to fetch water for the table, Rose scrolled through her recent text messages from Katie. She'd been *more* than surprised to learn that Rose was planning to stay on for another two weeks. But had said very little about it. And since then, her daily *How's it going?* texts had become more and more sparse.

Katie and Rose had known one another almost their entire lives, and Rose knew that Katie sensed something. Perhaps not the Thomas kind of something. But something that wasn't quite right.

With only three days left until she was due to return home, the pressure of wondering what she'd say when she saw Katie – it was okay trying to hide her feelings for Thomas by text but in person it would be almost impossible – and the creeping dread at actually having to leave Thomas behind were starting to make her feel tearful.

As she'd done so many times before, almost intuitively knowing that Rose was thinking of her, Katie's name lit up her phone.

I MISS YOU.

That was all the message said. And then Rose couldn't hold back her tears any longer. Ducking her head so the rest of the table didn't see her eyes starting to water, she got up and scurried back to her cabin. Then she buried her face in her pillow and cried.

When Thomas returned from his all-day trek, Rose told him she wasn't feeling too good and that, instead of drinking hot chocolate with him on the patio, she was going to get an early night.

She could tell by the look on his face that he felt there was something she wasn't telling him. But he didn't say anything, just squeezed her arm, kissed her forehead and headed back to the ranch house.

Thomas inhabited three rooms above the main building, which Rose still hadn't seen, and she couldn't help wondering what he was doing up there.

She was about to turn off the light and go to sleep when she heard a small tap-tap on the windows. Almost smiling, she opened the curtains and, of course, there he was.

Standing on the other side of the wall, Thomas gestured to the flask he'd put on the wall and as Rose opened the doors he called, "I'll just leave it. I'm not interrupting. I'm giving you space. I promise."

Rose smiled. She couldn't make him leave. Leaning on the wall with his elbows, grinning cheekily at her from beneath his beard – the beard she now knew felt surprisingly soft beneath her fingers – he was the most handsome guy she'd ever seen. Certainly the most handsome she'd ever dated.

"I did also bring you this, though..." Thomas reached behind his back and revealed a large bar of chocolate.

"Thank you," she said, stepping closer, taking it and opening it straight away. "Would you like a piece?"

Thomas lifted his hands and shook his head. "No, no. I'll leave you alone. I just–" He paused. "You seem a little down. Are you okay?"

Rose was standing on her side of the wall, her fingers touching Thomas'. "I'm fine," she said softly.

"Is that a real *fine* or a saying you're fine but you're not really fine kind of fine?"

"The second one, I think." Rose sighed and looked up, scared to meet his eyes because it always made her want to kiss him.

Thomas' brow furrowed into a frown. "Okay, I'm hopping over," he said, jumping over the wall and ushering her towards a chair by the unlit firepit.

Laughing, Rose allowed him to pull her onto his lap and wrap a blanket around them both.

"Right. Tell me. What's going on?"

"It's nothing."

"You literally just said it wasn't nothing." Thomas

narrowed his eyes at her then tilted his head. "Ah. I think I know what's going on."

"You do?"

"Mmm. Is this because I called you my girlfriend?" Thomas paused, searching her face, then spoke unusually quickly – as if he was trying to back-track. "Because it just slipped out. I didn't mean to freak you out. I just–"

"So, you didn't mean it?" Rose's hand was resting on Thomas' chest and she could feel his heartbeat quickening.

"If I did, would that be okay?"

Rose closed her eyes and breathed out slowly. "That's the problem, Thomas. I don't know."

"Rose, listen, it's okay. If you don't like me the way I like you, it's fine. I'm a big boy. I can handle it."

Rose frowned at him. She felt as if he was speaking Italian because she was struggling to comprehend what he'd said. "Wait. You think I don't like you as much as you like me?" She almost laughed.

"Honestly, it's okay. I mean, you're heading home in three days. I knew that from the beginning. *And* you're Katie's best friend, which obviously isn't good. I know it's been on your mind. I just figured..."

"What?" Rose had accidentally slipped her poker-face on and wasn't giving away the fact that, inside, her stomach was doing cartwheels.

Thomas pursed his lips, then stroked his beard. Was he blushing? "I figured that when you haven't found a girl you like in about a million years, if one comes along, you go for it. You don't chicken out."

"So, you like me?"

Thomas laughed and shook his head, then slipped his arms around her waist. "Yes. I like you. And I called you my girlfriend because you *feel* like my girlfriend. I look forward to seeing you every morning. I think about you every night. I like you, Rose. A lot."

Rose felt her lips spread into a giant grin. "I like you too."

"So why'd you go into hermit mode this evening? Why'd you try and hide away from me?"

"Because I like you too much, Thomas. I'm terrified by how much I like you. Katie explicitly warned me *not* to fall for you because you'd break my heart." Again, she felt tears biting at the backs of her eyes. "And I have to leave you in three days, and tell her, and..." She began to sniff as tears rolled down her cheeks. "And it's all a disaster."

Thomas laughed. A great big, soft, warm laugh that made Rose want to nuzzle into his neck and never leave him. "Rose, it is definitely not a disaster. I promise. It's too wonderful to be a disaster."

And then he kissed her.

And the tears stopped.

CHAPTER 19

When Thomas stopped kissing her, he smiled and cupped her face in his hands. Then he frowned. "So, why did Katie think I'd break your heart?"

Rose laughed, remembering all the times she'd worried about Thomas and Fleur, all the times she thought he couldn't possibly like her and was just being friendly. And then, although she was trying not to, she remembered what Fleur had said about Thomas not being the 'girl-friend' type. She looked away, unsure whether she should tell him.

"Well?" He raised his eyebrows at her.

"Well, Katie said that you're not really the commit-ment type. She said you have a different girlfriend every week." Rose winced as she said it, watching Thomas' face carefully to see how he'd react.

"Wow. Did she?"

"Mmm. And Fleur..."

"Fleur?" Thomas' eyes widened and a tiny flicker of annoyance crossed his face.

"It was nothing. She just made a comment about you not really being the kind of guy who had girlfriends – serious girlfriends, I mean. And after what Katie said, I guess it–"

"Made you think I'm a bit of a player?"

Rose tried to lighten the mood by smiling and playfully stroking Thomas' beard. "I think *cad* was the word Katie used."

"I thought she was joking about that," Thomas mused, biting the corner of his lip. He really did look hurt by the idea. "Listen, Rose," he said, very seriously. "I haven't been the girlfriend type because I've never met anyone I like enough to want as a girlfriend. It's as simple as that."

Rose tried to stop herself from grinning as her heart began to race.

"But with you..." He leaned in and pressed his forehead against hers. "It's different. Totally different."

There was silence for a moment and then Rose whispered, "It's different for me too. I've never really felt like this before, Thomas. To be honest, it's kind of terrifying."

Thomas laughed softly and wrapped his arms around her.

"I'm leaving in three days." Rose held her breath, waiting for him to reply.

"I know."

"So," she said. "What do we do?"

"Enjoy it?" Thomas whispered, nibbling at her ear.

Rose smiled. At least, she tried to smile. But it didn't quite reach her lips. Deep down, she'd been hoping Thomas would say, *We'll be okay. Long distance relationships can work. We'll email and video chat. I'll fly to England and you can fly out here and then one day...* But he hadn't. He'd said, *Enjoy it.*

"I guess you're right," she said, still not smiling. Then she patted him on the arm, trying to brighten her expression. "But if I don't want to look like a total zombie tomorrow, I need some sleep. So, I'll see you in the morning?" She slid off his lap and stood up, the blanket that had been wrapped around them falling loosely over Thomas' shoulders.

"Sure." He stood up too. "Actually, I've got a surprise for you tomorrow."

"You have?" There was the flicker again. The one that always managed to push her doubts aside or drown them out.

"Mm hmm. I'll be back at seven with coffee." Thomas swung his legs over the wall and landed softly on the other side. "Goodnight, Rose."

"Goodnight, Thomas."

Thomas' surprise was completely unexpected, which – admittedly – was the whole point of a surprise. But Rose was usually quite good at figuring them out. The next morning, however, when he arrived at her cabin with a backpack and told her to pack some overnight clothes, she was almost speechless.

"Overnight?"

Thomas nodded. "You, Rose Parker, are going on your very first trek."

"A trek?" Rose's mouth hung open. "Thomas, the most I've done is ride up and down the paddock."

"Which is why it is a really special trek. A beginner's trek with your own personal one-to-one guide."

"And I need overnight things because..?"

"Because we'll be riding to one of the most beautiful spots in the whole of Tuscany and camping out under the stars," he said, gesturing up to the sky and then wiggling his eyebrows at her.

Rose breathed in deeply, trying to figure out whether she was feeling sick with excitement or nerves.

"You'll be riding Mass, and he knows these routes really well. So, you'll be absolutely, totally, one-hundred percent safe."

The mention of Massimo made her smile. "Okay," she said, resolutely. "I guess I've got this far. I might as well push myself one last bit."

Softening, the way he always did when he was trying to make her feel better, Thomas leaned in. "You will be absolutely fine. And I'll be with you the whole time."

Rose nodded. "Okay, how long do I have to get ready?"

"An hour?"

Rose took the flask of coffee he'd set down on the wall and turned back to her cabin. "Right. See you in an hour then."

As they walked down towards the stables, following the now-familiar path from the ranch house, Rose looped her arm through Thomas' and leaned into his shoulder. "So, you said you're going to be my *personal* riding instructor?"

"Mm hmm." Thomas smiled cheekily at her.

"Which means this trek is just you and me? For two whole days and one whole night?"

Thomas nodded, clearly trying not to grin too widely.

"But, how? Aren't you already short staffed. How are they going to cope without you? And I know I'm not a massive help but without me in the stables in the morning, that's going to be a lot of pressure on the others."

Thomas squeezed her shoulder. "It'll be fine. It's handover weekend so we've got a bunch of groups leaving today and a bunch of new ones arriving tomorrow. No treks or lessons, just waving people off and settling them in."

"Ah, then it's perfect timing."

Thomas tapped his forehead with his index finger. "Not just a pretty face, you know."

Down at the stables, Massimo and Stella were already waiting for them, saddled up and ready to go, and Rose surprised herself by climbing up onto Massimo's back with relative ease and precision.

Thomas seemed impressed too because, sitting beside her, already comfortable in Stella's saddle, he grinned. "Would you have believed you'd be doing this if I'd have told you three weeks ago?"

"Absolutely not," Rose laughed. But then she leaned down and stroked Massimo's mane. "You'll look after me, though, Mass. Won't you?"

As if in agreement, Massimo dipped his head and whinnied. And then Thomas said, "Right, are you ready for your first trek?"

Rose breathed in deeply through her nose, counted to three and breathed out again. "Ready as I'll ever be."

CHAPTER 20

From the stables, they headed through one of the larger paddocks and out the other side.

Rose had never ventured into this part of the ranch before and it felt like she was seeing a side of Thomas' life that he'd, so far, kept hidden.

For at least twenty minutes, they didn't speak. The path, which ran beside a row of bushes, was narrow and bumpy. At first, Rose felt very uneasy; she was used to riding Massimo around grassy paddocks where the ground was level, so the swaying and jostling of Mass' body as he navigated his way over the uneven parts of the path made her feel like she might suddenly be dislodged from her seat.

After a while, though, she realised that Massimo knew exactly what he was doing and where he was going. With

Stella and Thomas in front, Rose barely needed to direct Massimo. She just needed to sit and hold on.

Every now and then, the horses stopped to nibble at some berries or some grass. And Rose soon realised that this was not going to be a quick march to a camp site but a long and leisurely day.

Glancing back at her, Thomas smiled. "You okay, back there?"

Rose nodded, trying to encourage Massimo to leave his latest berry hoard and move on. "So, where are we headed?" she asked, loudly, so that her voice would reach Thomas.

"Rose, it's not about the destination," he called back. "It's just about enjoying the ride."

Rose laughed.

"Bit of a cliché, but true," he replied.

An hour later, finally making their way out of the small pathways that enclosed the ranch, they emerged into a forest. Here, the paths were wide enough for them to ride side by side. Sunlight fell through the branches, dancing on the ground in front of them. And, out of the glare of the Italian summer sun, it was refreshingly cool.

"I can see why you love doing this all day," she said as she looked up at the canopy above them.

Thomas sighed. "It's hard work. The ranch. But this is the reward."

Rose pictured her own job, back in England. And suddenly the thought of her desk, and her computer, and the little brown cubicle with no natural daylight that she sat in for ten hours a day, filled her with dread. "It's amazing." She pursed her lips and looked away from Thomas so he couldn't see her face. "You're amazing, Thomas. You carved out this life for yourself and it's just..."

"Just?"

"I don't know." Rose shrugged. "It just makes my life seem so horribly dull. I can't imagine going back to it." She glanced at him then quickly added, "I mean, I'm sure it'll be fine. Once I'm back, I'll be fine. It's just, right now, it seems a million miles away."

Thomas reached out and patted her leg. "Well, why don't we pretend that it is? Just forget about it for two whole days and enjoy this." He widened his arms and looked at their surroundings.

"Yes," she said, "let's."

For the rest of the day, Thomas and Rose rode through the woods and hills beyond the ranch. A couple of times, they emerged into a wide-open space that offered incredible views of the landscape beyond. Other times, the paths became narrow and more shaded by trees and bushes.

They stopped and ate lunch at a small, deserted picnic area; Thomas produced a bag of freshly made bread and Italian specialities from Mama Tina's kitchen back at the ranch and, as they ate, Rose felt like suddenly she could imagine what Thomas did all day when he took the guests out for their treks.

"I like this," she said, smiling at him.

"Her food is amazing, isn't it? When Burt left me the ranch, I practically begged her to stay. It wouldn't have been the same without her."

Rose, mouth half-full, nodded in agreement. "The food *is* amazing, but I meant this." She waved her hand at the trees around them, then reached out to take Thomas' hand. "Being with you. Seeing this side of your life."

"I haven't kept it from you, Rose. I'd have loved you to come out sooner. I just didn't want to push you—"

"Oh, I know, I know." She squeezed his hand, then lifted it and kissed his knuckles.

Thomas wrinkled his nose at her, clearly enjoying her being more affectionate than usual.

"I should have," she said, quietly. "I'm sorry I didn't."

"You're here now." Thomas leaned forward over the picnic table and planted a kiss on her nose.

Rose smiled. But, inside, she couldn't ignore the voice that was shouting, *Not here for long, though. Are you? Soon, he'll be doing this without you. You'll be hundreds of miles away and Thomas will still be here. Will he miss you? Will he pine for you?*

Shaking her head and starting to pack away some of the picnic things, Rose looked over at Massimo. "Do they need some water?"

"They do. We'll head down to the river." Thomas took

the backpack from Rose and then helped her up onto Massimo's back. "Ready?"

She reached down and patted Massimo's neck. "I don't know. Are you ready, boy?" Then she sat up. "Yep, he's ready."

"Oh, you talk to horses now, do you? Remarkable Rose."

"Only ones I like."

Thomas grinned. "Never thought I'd hear you say that you liked a horse."

"Well," she said. "I had a great coach."

Down by the river, they stopped to let the horses drink. It was wide and slow moving, winding its way through the trees and out of sight.

"On the advanced treks, we cross the river here and then follow it up to the waterfall. I'll show you some pictures. It's my favourite one."

"I'd like that." Rose fidgeted in her saddle and glanced over to the other side of the river. "How far away is the waterfall?"

"Only about an hour from here. On the overnights, we camp there then head back the next day."

"Maybe we could..." Rose trailed off, widening her eyes at him. The thought of camping out beside a waterfall with Thomas made her feel a little giddy.

Thomas smiled but shook his head, touching his beard the way he did when he was thinking. "Rose, I would *love* to take you there. But..." He paused, as if he was trying to think of a polite way to phrase what he wanted to say next. "I don't think you're ready," he said, tentatively. "It really is an advanced route. There are steep slopes to navigate – you have to dismount and walk the horse down them. And we usually gallop across the fields to make it quicker." He reached out and patted her leg. "Next time you come, yeah?"

Thomas nudged Stella with the heels of his boots and was turning her around to head back to the path they'd left when Rose suddenly, without even thinking about it, bent down and whispered to Massimo, "Let's show him what we can do, Mass."

Thomas didn't have chance to anticipate what she was doing and, by the time he'd realised, she and Massimo were standing in the middle of the shallow river. Rose grinned and waved at him. "Come and get me, Goodwin!"

Thomas laughed, but then something else flashed across his face and he became very, very serious. "Rose, that's not a good idea. Come on."

"Seriously. I can do it, Thomas. Mass looks like he knows the way. So, are you coming with us?" A fizzing, tingling, thudding feeling had flooded her chest and she felt almost intoxicated with bravado. She could do this. She'd faced her fears, she'd played midwife to a horse in labour, she'd mucked out stables, she learned to ride and –

Thomas said so himself – proved to be quite a natural at it. And if this was their last chance to spend time together, time that Thomas would remember, she needed to prove to him that she could fit in with his life here. Make it so that he could imagine her returning.

Thomas was shaking his head, inching Stella closer but clearly expecting Rose to cave in and return.

"Okay," she said, waving. "See you!" And then she tapped Massimo's sides and he dutifully walked on.

If they'd been anywhere else, Thomas probably would have cantered to catch up with her. But the river wouldn't allow it. Behind her, Rose could hear Stella's heavy legs splashing through the water. But she didn't turn around. And when she reached the bank on the other side, she whispered to Mass, "Okay, boy. You know the way. Lead on."

As if he understood her, completely, Massimo continued. And Rose could just about make out the path they were following. It was narrow. On either side, branches brushed against her skin. Behind, Thomas called, "Rose. Please, listen." He sounded cross. But, somehow, it just made her more determined to prove him wrong. "This isn't a joke, Rose. Come on."

"Thomas, I can do this," she shouted. "It's no different from the paths we were on a while back."

"Rose. Stop." Thomas' voice sounded panicked and, for a moment, Rose wondered whether she should listen. But she always listened. She was always sensible. Today, right now, she needed to be brave. She needed to be *remarkable* Rose. Not timid, *does-as-she's-told* Rose.

"Okay. That's it. I need you to stop. There's a–"

Thomas' voice disappeared. Suddenly, she wasn't in the woods anymore. She was at the top of a sheer, rocky drop that went down and down. Rose sat back in her seat and pulled on the reins, expecting Massimo to stop.

But he didn't. He trekked forwards. Rose shrieked.

"Rose! Stop! You need to dismount and lead him down." Thomas was almost screaming at her.

But it was too late. Massimo was already heading down, gingerly placing his hooves one after the other.

"Sit back in the seat. Balance his weight!"

Rose looked back. Thomas was standing beside Stella, holding onto her reins, slipping and sliding as he helped her navigate the rocks. He looked at the horse, then at Rose. "I can't leave her, Rose."

"I'm okay," she said, trembling. "I'm okay. Massimo's okay." But, just as she said it, Massimo's front legs wobbled. Rose felt like they were going to collapse, the pair of them, and tumble down the hillside. But he righted himself.

They were almost at the bottom, and she could see the ground flattening out in front of them, becoming a wide open space, become safe, when a noise shattered the silence around them. A short, sharp *crack*. And then another. So loud it made the hillside vibrate.

Rose's heart was racing. She reached forward and was

about to whisper to Massimo and tell him everything was okay but then there was another *crack,* much louder, much closer. And he reared up on his hind legs.

Clinging on to the reins and gripping the saddle with her thighs, Rose managed not to fall.

But then Massimo bolted.

CHAPTER 21

*R*ose heard herself scream as Massimo broke into a gallop and sped across the field in front of them. She was struggling to hold on. She was going to fall. She was going to fall and break her neck and she'd never see Thomas or Katie or her family ever again.

She tried to think. Tried to think what she should do but she couldn't. She was shouting, "Mass, it's okay. Slow down, slow down." But he wasn't listening.

She was trying to tug on the reins to tell him to stop but she couldn't. Every time she moved she felt like she was going to lose her grip.

Then suddenly, Thomas was beside her. Stella was galloping alongside Massimo, so close they were almost touching. Thomas let go of Stella's reins, magically staying upright and in the saddle, leaning over.

"Rose, let go of the reins and hold on to his saddle."

Rose, trembling, did as he instructed.

Thomas reached out and grabbed Massimo's reins.

Rose closed her eyes. She felt sick, and terrified, and stupid all at the same time. But, gradually, they began to slow down. Massimo began to slow down. The thunder of hooves on grass petered out. They were trotting. Walking. Still.

She had barely opened her eyes before Thomas was grabbing hold of her and pulling her down from the saddle. She winced. Her heart was racing so hard she felt like it might burst from her rib cage. Her legs wobbled. She looked up, expecting Thomas to be furious. But instead he was holding her face in his hands and smoothing her hair and then pulling her to his chest.

"Are you all right? Are you okay?"

Unable to fight back the tears that were coming, Rose sunk down to the floor and Thomas knelt beside her. "I'm so sorry," she whispered. "I'm so sorry."

Thomas shook his head, then the smallest flicker of a smile danced across his lips. "What were you thinking?"

Rose tried to laugh, but it came out as a sob. "I don't know. I really don't know. I just..." Her words were coming out in breathless bursts. "I wanted you to think I was remarkable."

Thomas' eyes were glistening. Was he crying too? Surely not. He shook his head, then pulled her close and wrapped his arms around her, kissing the top of her head. "Rose. I thought you were remarkable the moment I met you. You don't need to hurl yourself off the side of a cliff to prove yourself to me."

"But..." Rose pulled back and looked up at him. "I just wanted you to have a really good memory of me. So you didn't forget me."

Thomas grinned at her. "I'd say it's mission accomplished, wouldn't you?"

Finally, the trembling and the nausea subsiding, Rose smiled too. "Not really what I was going for."

Thomas shook his head at her. "But memorable. Definitely memorable."

Sinking back and leaning against him, Rose sighed and wiped her eyes. "What was that noise? What frightened him?"

"There's a farm over that way. They shoot out here sometimes. *Usually,* we tell them when we're coming up here on a trek and they make sure not to be doing it. You know," Thomas said, giving her a pointed look, "so the horses don't get spooked and, say, bolt."

"Ah."

"Mmm hmm."

"Poor Mass. I'm so sorry."

Thomas squeezed her and kissed her head again. "Well, now that we're most of the way there, we might as well carry on and camp by the waterfall. What do you reckon?"

Rose laughed and bit her lower lip. "I mean, I feel like you're rewarding me for my terrible behaviour. But, yes.

That would be lovely." She paused and looked at her legs, which still felt both numb and wobbly at the same time. "I might need a minute before I can stand though."

"Minute granted," said Thomas, sighing and resting his chin on the top of her head. "I think my heart needs a while to calm down too."

Two hours later, after a very slow walk, they arrived at the foot of the small woodland waterfall. Below it sat a glistening pool surrounded by rocks and a small clearing where Thomas set up their tent and lit a campfire.

While he worked, Rose sat and watched him. She had been unbelievably foolish. She had risked her life and Thomas' and put the horses in danger, just because she wanted to impress him. And now, despite the fact he'd tried to make her feel better about it and hadn't yelled or been angry, she felt as if deep down he must be convinced that she was *not* the girl for him.

Finally finished, Thomas sat down beside her and took off his hat. "Okay," he said. "Now we can relax."

Fiddling with her hair, Rose glanced at him and then looked down at her feet. "Thomas," she whispered. "Why are you being so nice to me?"

Thomas frowned at her. "You thought I'd be *not* nice?"

"No, but I did do something pretty stupid."

Thomas tilted his head. "You did. But I think you've learned your lesson."

Rose sighed. "Do you think I'm ridiculous?"

For a moment, Thomas didn't say anything. But then he nudged closer to her and put his hands on her upper arms, turning her so that she was facing him. "Rose. It kind of bothers me that you don't seem to get how much I like you. Is it because of what Katie and Fleur said? Is all that stuff still bothering you? Because–"

"No. It's not that." Rose smiled a thin smile. "Don't you get it?"

"Get what?"

"Look at you," she said, laughing. "I mean, you wear some questionable footwear, but apart from that you're a ten. And I'm, like, a four. Maybe."

Thomas' eyes widened, but then they narrowed into a frown. "Okay. Wow. So, first of all, I had no idea you hated my boots. That hurts." He laughed, but then straightened his expression into something much more serious. "But, Rose, don't you get it? To me, you're a ten *plus*. You're..." He sighed and scraped his fingers through his hair. Then reached into his pocket and took out his phone. Holding it so she could see, he unlocked the screen and showed it to her.

His background photo was a selfie that they'd taken down at the stables. Rose was wearing his hat and they were both in red T-shirts. Rose was grinning. Thomas was kissing her cheek.

"You know what I see when I look at that?" Thomas wiggled the phone at her.

Rose shook her head.

"I see the most beautiful woman in the world letting me kiss her. And it makes me feel like the luckiest guy who ever lived." Handing her the phone, he added, "Look at that and tell me we don't look *awesome* together."

Rose smiled at the picture, touching it lightly with her index finger. "It's not just that," she said softly. "I guess I just wanted to prove to you that I can be brave and impressive. That I'd fit in here."

"But you've already proved that! You *are* all those things."

Rose sniffed and wiped her eyes with the back of her hand.

"Listen. I get it. When I was younger, before I came here, I was so shy. You remember. I found being in groups really tough. I didn't know what to say around people. I was always self-conscious, always anxious. And it wasn't like some magical transformation happened the second I set foot on the ranch."

"It wasn't?"

Thomas laughed a shallow laugh and shook his head. "No." Clearing his throat, he added, "No one here knows this. They'd never let me live it down."

"What?"

"It took me about three months to be able to climb up into the saddle without sliding right off again."

Rose frowned at him. "You're just saying that."

"Afraid not. It was *awful*. I used to practise at night, on this great big metal barrel they used for beginners. I just couldn't do it. Didn't have the coordination or the upper body strength."

"I thought you said that Burt told you you were a natural?"

"He did. After I actually managed to get up on the horse and stay there for more than thirty seconds." Thomas tweaked his index finger under Rose's chin and smiled at her. "So, you see. I really do get it."

Rose tried to picture Thomas falling off his horse. It seemed utterly unbelievable.

But then she remembered the Thomas Goodwin she used to know; the one who'd been shy and spotty and so nice to talk to. And, suddenly, it all fell into place. The old Thomas merged with the new Thomas and she realised exactly why she went to bits around him. Why she'd fallen so hard and so fast. Why he sent her giddy when he walked into a room; because she knew that beneath his crazy good looks was a big, warm heart, and a stupid sense of humour, and a guy who'd always actually listened to her. Who had always seen her. Even when no-one else did.

Taking a deep breath in, Rose leaned forward and placed her hands lightly on Thomas' shoulders, letting her arms loop around his neck as she pressed her lips against his.

When she pulled away, he looked surprised but was smiling.

"I have an idea," she said.

"Not another one. I think you've had enough good ideas for one day, don't you?"

"How about a swim?"

Thomas looked at the water, then at Rose. "Actually, that's an idea I can get on board with."

A few hours later, after swimming fully clothed in the pool beneath the waterfall, Thomas and Rose sat beside one another, huddled under a blanket.

They'd changed into fresh clothes from their backpacks. Pyjamas. Which Rose found both odd and lovely at the same time. And now they were eating toasted marshmallows and watching the flames of their campfire flicker up into the air.

"Thank you for an exhilarating day," Thomas said, nudging Rose's arm.

Rose hung her head and tutted at herself. "I still can't believe I was so reckless."

"Be honest – the whole thing was planned wasn't it? You wanted to see me leap into action and rescue you like a damsel in distress."

"I don't think anyone has ever called me a *damsel* before. But, as much as I probably shouldn't admit it..."

She wriggled closer to Thomas and tucked herself under his arm. "It was pretty nice being rescued."

Thomas laughed, lifted a marshmallow from the fire and handed it to her. Rose took the stick it was attached to and started to pick at it, enjoying the way it was both soft and crispy at the same time.

She was still licking marshmallow goo from her fingers when Thomas abruptly stood up. Holding out his hand as if they were at a high school dance, he said, very formally, "Rose, would you care to dance?"

Rose looked around, half-expecting to see a band jump out from behind the trees. "Thomas, we don't have any music."

"Ah." He raised a finger at her then went over to the tent. When he returned, he was holding a small plug-in speaker and his phone. "Any requests?" he asked, smiling.

"Surprise me."

Rose got up and stood with her hands behind her back, swaying on the balls of her feet, waiting for Thomas to press play. When he did, she laughed. It was a song that used to play at the end of their school dances. A cheesy slow-dance with horrible lyrics. But when Thomas reached for her hand a second time, she took it.

Thomas twirled her into the middle of the clearing and pulled her close, wrapping both arms around her waist while she looped hers around his neck.

As they swayed together, the sun finally disappeared and the clearing darkened. Above, stars decorated the sky.

Beside them, the fire flickered and crackled. And Rose felt as if she was quite possibly the happiest she'd ever been in her life.

"Thomas," she whispered, resting her head on his shoulder.

"Rose?"

"I don't want to go home. I don't want this to end."

Thomas was stroking her back. He kissed her head and whispered back, "Neither do I."

"Maybe it doesn't have to," she said, softly. "Maybe we could make it work. Figure out how to tell Katie. I know long distance isn't great but–"

Thomas stopped and leaned back so that he was looking at her. "If we want it to work, Rose. It will work."

Rose smiled. A big, elated smile. "You really mean that?"

"I'm not going to let you slip away, Rose." Thomas tightened his grip on her and nuzzled into her neck. "You're too remarkable to let go of."

CHAPTER 22

*A*rriving back at the ranch late the following afternoon, after spending the morning lounging by their tent and swimming beneath the waterfall, Rose almost expected a fan fare; it felt as if they'd been gone for weeks. But no one at the stables really even noticed them. Chris said a quick, "Hi," as he crossed the yard. Mike waved. And everyone else just carried on as normal.

Climbing out of Massimo's saddle and handing him over to Allison, who offered to see to both him and Stella, Rose was struck by the sudden realisation that this could be the last time she actually rode. Until she returned, of course.

"Will there be time to ride tomorrow morning?" she asked, sliding her arm through Thomas' as they walked up towards the ranch house.

Thomas didn't smile, like he usually did, but swallowed hard and bit his lower lip. "What time's your flight? I'd been trying to forget about it."

"Mid-day."

"It'll be pushing it. I'll get your cab to come at eight so we'd need to ride at six thirty. Probably just a quick turn around the paddock."

"Sounds great." Rose tried to look excited. But now they were back and her departure was a reality, she felt suddenly and overwhelmingly sad.

"I'll come get you at six and we'll walk down together." Thomas smiled, hugging her in closer to his waist.

"Maybe this evening we can think about when I might be able to come back?" Rose asked tentatively. "I won't have many vacation days left this year but if you came to England in a few months, I could probably make it for a weekend closer to Christmas and..." She trailed off because Thomas was chewing his lip as if he didn't really want to talk about it.

"Let's see how it goes, yeah? We don't need to plan it right now, do we?"

Rose blinked hard and tried to force a smile. Last night, Thomas had talked as if they were now 'official'. As if he couldn't wait for her to come back. As if they'd talk every night and do video chats and tell Katie about it and it would all be fine. But now he seemed like he didn't want to discuss it.

Sighing, because he was probably finding it hard too, Rose slipped her hand into his and asked if he fancied a swim to cool down from the ride. "You know, you never did show me the before and after photos of the pool," she said, nudging him playfully.

"Ah, well there we go then." Thomas brightened and smiled at her. "That's our last night all planned out. Dinner and a slide show."

"Perfect."

Later, however, after they ate dinner in the hall with the others and walked slowly back towards Rose's cabin, Thomas did not offer to show her pictures of the renovation. He didn't even offer to stay and talk and spend just a few last, precious hours together.

"Sorry, Rose. I need to go make some calls. Things that weren't sorted while I was gone."

Rose was standing on her side of the wall and Thomas on the other. Her heart tugged and her stomach lurched, as if she'd just gone over the peak of a rollercoaster and was tumbling downwards. Where had the affectionate, sparkly Thomas from last night disappeared to?

"Oh. I thought..." She looked behind her at the chairs and the fire pit. "Will you come back after?"

"Probably best we get an early night. I'll see you in the morning though, for our last ride?"

Rose flinched. He'd said 'last'. Did this mean there wouldn't ever be another one? Almost shaking her head, she tried to wriggle free from her paranoia. Last night, Thomas had told her she was the best thing that had ever happened to him. So, maybe he was feeling just as sad as she was and this was simply his way of processing it. Smiling gently, trying to make him see that she was feeling the same, Rose took his hand and leaned over to kiss him.

Thomas kissed her back. A slow, different kind of kiss that she didn't quite understand. "Goodnight, Rose."

"Goodnight."

That night, Rose barely slept. After packing her case, she waited outside just in case Thomas changed his mind and returned. Then she texted him. Three times. But he didn't reply.

Something was going on. She could feel it. But she had no idea what it was.

At five a.m., she decided enough was enough. Enough moping. And enough expecting Thomas to always be the one making romantic gestures. On their last morning together, she decided *she* would bring *him* coffee for a change.

So, leaving her packed bags and her hand luggage behind in the cabin, Rose ventured up to the ranch house, slipped into the dining hall and filled two takeaway cups with strong black coffee.

They weren't the jolly blue flasks that Thomas usually carried, but it was the thought that counted.

Glancing at her reflection, she smiled. Thomas would be surprised, she knew he would. And then she'd see him twinkle at her again and they would enjoy a few more blissful hours together before she had to get in the cab and leave.

Leaving through the doors to the terrace, Rose headed around to the back of the ranch house. She'd never seen inside Thomas' living quarters but she knew the stairs to his apartment were down near the kitchen gardens.

She rounded the corner, smiling and holding her coffee cups, and then stopped dead in her tracks.

At the bottom of the steps that led up to Thomas' rooms, two figures were embracing. Two figures she recognised.

Thomas and Fleur.

Rose stepped back into the shadow of the building. Her throat was constricting so hard that she felt she might hyperventilate.

As they broke apart, Thomas smiled. And then Fleur reached up on her tip-toes, stroked his cheek, and kissed him.

Rose almost let out a muffled cry. But, slamming her hand over her mouth and dropping the coffee to the ground, she stopped herself.

She turned, biting her lower lip and pleading with herself not to cry. Then she ran back to the front of the building.

She was on the terrace, panting and trying to slow down her thoughts, trying to think of some way - any way -

that what she saw could be interpreted as something else, when a hand touched her shoulder.

She whirled around, ready to shout at Thomas, *What was that?!* But it wasn't Thomas.

"Rossi?" Rose's cheeks were flushed and her voice came out much louder than she'd intended.

Rossi smiled at her casually and in his soft Italian accent said, "Rose. Is everything all right?"

"What are you doing here?" she asked, looking behind him as if she might see Thomas and Fleur emerging sheepishly from behind the building.

"Just delivering some medicines to the stables." Rossi frowned at her. "Are you okay, Rose?"

"Rossi, are you leaving?"

Rossi frowned some more. "I am."

"Now?"

"I'm on my way back to my truck."

"Can you give me a lift into town?"

"A lift?"

"I need to leave. My flight's at midday but I want to leave now."

Rossi's eyes widened as if he finally understood what she was saying. "Of course. I can take you to Diamo. There's a train that goes straight to the airport from there."

"Thank you," Rose smiled, nodding, finding her breath again. "Thank you. I'll go grab my things."

"I'll meet you at the truck," Rossi said, still watching

her as if he knew there was something she wasn't saying but had decided not to pry.

And so Rose ran back to her cabin, grabbed her bags, and without taking a second glance at the patio or the fire pit or the chairs where she and Thomas had talked until the early hours of the morning, she left.

CHAPTER 23

When Rose got to the airport and through the baggage check into the departure lounge, she finally turned on her phone. Thomas had called her twenty-five times but, looking at the notifications, she felt completely numb.

As Rossi had driven her away from the ranch, it was as if everything had slowly come into focus. Katie had been right. Everything Thomas said was a lie. He'd used her and she'd fallen for it. But she wasn't going to give him the chance to win her round. She was done.

After queueing for fifteen minutes to buy a coffee, Rose found somewhere to sit down. Rather than Thomas, all she could think about was Katie.

She'd risked their friendship for nothing.

And now she was going to have to find a way to tell her.

Quickly, before she had a chance to back out, Rose scrolled to Katie's name and pressed 'call'.

"Katie?"

"Rose! Where are you?"

Katie sounded worried. "I'm at the airport. Katie, there's something I–"

"You're at the airport? How? Katie, Thomas is worried sick – he said you just disappeared."

"You spoke to him?"

Katie paused, then said, "Listen, Rose. Thomas told me about the two of you."

Rose felt a lump form in her throat. "Katie," she breathed, putting her head in her hands. "I'm so sorry. I'm so, so sorry. You were right. About all of it. I fell for him. I thought he liked me. I thought I was different from the other girls he'd dated. He told me I was. But then this morning I–"

"Rose – stop. Slow down." Katie didn't sound angry. Her voice was soft, almost as if she was smiling. "I'm not mad."

"You're not?"

"Don't get me wrong. I was. When Tommy told me I was furious at the pair of you. I couldn't believe he had gone after you and I couldn't believe you hadn't told me."

Rose began to reply but Katie interrupted her.

"But then he texted me last night and explained. And now I get it."

Rose frowned. Her brain was struggling to make sense of what Katie was saying. "Get what?"

"I get that it's serious between you."

Rose shook her head. "Katie, I don't know what he said to you but—"

"Rose. I'm sorry. I'm at work and I have to go. But I'm going to send you the text he sent to me last night. Clearly something's happened between you but, for once, I think I'm on Tommy's side. I'll send it now. I love you. Bye."

Rose stared at the phone. Katie had hung up. She'd been totally fine with it and then she'd just hung up. Rose felt as if she was in some kind of twisted, parallel universe.

A few seconds later, Katie's text pinged through. Rose opened it. It was long. Way longer than a normal text. And she almost felt as if she shouldn't be reading it. But she needed an explanation. She needed to understand why Thomas would have bothered teling his sister about them if he wasn't serious about it. If, the whole time, he'd been seeing Fleur behind her back. Or if he was going to be so easily swayed that he'd end up kissing someone else before Rose had even left the ranch.

So, taking a deep breath, she made herself read.

K, I know you're mad and don't want to talk to me. But I need to explain.

Firstly, please don't be angry with Rose. It's eaten her up that she hasn't been open with you. She's hated every second of it and I never, ever want to come between you two.

But, secondly, I promise – seriously, like, the most serious I've ever been about anything – that I really, really like her.

I always kind of liked her when we were kids. But, you know, we didn't really know each other that well. And then when I saw her get out of the cab with you. I don't know, my heart just did this somersault and I was hooked. I couldn't stay away from her even when I tried.

I know you think I'm a total commitment-phobe. And, yeah, you're right, I've never had a real relationship. But that's because no one has ever got me the way Rose does.

She's amazing, Katie. So amazing that I want to ask her to stay with me. Here on the ranch. She's leaving tomorrow morning and she might say no and break my heart, but I need to ask her.

And I can't do that until I know it's okay with you. Until I know you won't be mad at her. I need to be able to tell her that you're happy for us. Then maybe, just maybe, she'll stay.

I know I'm a pain. And I know we don't really do 'feelings' – you and me – but I'm your big brother, K. And I'm telling you the truth.

I think Rose is 'The One'.

Call me.

Tommy xxx

"Please, I need to get out of the airport."

"Ma'am. I'm sorry. You cannot go back once you're in the departure lounge."

"It's an emergency!" Rose was pleading with a tall, thick-set security guard. But he was *not* giving in. Clutching her phone in her hand, the words in Thomas' text were burned into her brain. He was going to ask her to stay. He'd called her 'The One'. So, whatever had happened with Fleur she at least needed to ask him face-to-face for an explanation. She couldn't just leave and never see him again. Not now.

"What kind of emergency? Are you sick?" The security guard folded and unfolded his arms.

"No, I'm not sick. I–"

"Rose?!"

She turned. She'd know his voice anywhere. "Thomas?"

And, like something from a Hollywood movie, there he was – striding through the crowd in the departure hall in his cowboy boots and ridiculous hat.

Rose was rooted to the spot. Her entire body stiffened, despite the voice in her head that was screaming, *Thomas, oh thank goodness, you came! You really came!*

"Rose!" He was out of breath, smiling, putting his hands on her arms. "I didn't know if I'd catch you. I had to buy a ticket... Pisa... three hundred Euro..."

Rose searched his face. She couldn't find the words she needed. She wanted to throw herself at him and never let go but at the same time all she could see was the way he'd embraced Fleur on the steps.

"What happened?" Thomas was shaking his head. "You didn't say goodbye? You just disappeared. Is it Katie? Because I spoke to her, Rose. I told her–"

"It's not Katie." Rose folded her arms in front of her chest, trying not to just instantly give in to him.

Thomas took off his hat. "Then... what?"

Rose exhaled slowly, trying to keep her voice calm, aware that they were surrounded by people who could hear them. "I saw you."

"Saw me..?"

"I saw you with Fleur. I saw you with your arms around her. I saw her..." Rose swallowed hard. "I saw her kiss you, Thomas." As she said it, and her eyes met his, she began to waver. She was determined not to cry but remembering what she saw, and how she felt in that moment, was making it extremely hard.

Thomas remained still, then his expression slid into something crumpled and worried-looking. He breathed out heavily, took his hat off and swept his fingers through his hair. "Rose..."

Rose sniffed and looked away, blinking up at the ceiling. "I don't want excuses, Thomas. Katie warned me from the start, didn't she? I was an idiot to–"

"Rose..." Thomas suddenly dropped his hat to the

ground and moved deftly towards her. One hand slid around her waist and the other was reaching up to sweep her hair from her face. "Rose..." He was whispering and it was making her want to cry and blush at the same time. She tried to pull away but Thomas met her eyes and said, slowly, "There is *nothing* between Fleur and I."

"Oh, she's just a bit of fun but I'm *special*? Is that it?" Rose shook her head but felt herself leaning into the warmth of his fingers on her cheek.

"You are special. Yes. You're the only girl I've ever..." Thomas swallowed hard and licked his lower lip. "Fleur was upset because Rossi broke up with her. I was being a friend, that's all."

"Rossi?"

Thomas nodded and rolled his eyes. "She's been chasing after him all summer. I knew they'd started seeing each other but it turns out it was just a fling for him and a bit more serious for her."

"But the *kiss* Thomas. I saw you—"

"You saw Fleur kiss me. But you obviously didn't stick around too long or you'd have seen what happened next."

"What happened next?"

Thomas leaned in closer, so that his forehead was almost touching hers. "You'd have seen me *stop* her. And you'd have heard me tell her that there is only one woman in the world who I want to be with."

"Oh." Rose was blinking back tears, but at the same time she could feel her lips spreading into a grin.

"And, I told Katie. I told her–"

"I know. I spoke to her–"

"Then you know – you know I told her that you're the only one for me, Rose. Not just the only one. *The* One."

"The One?"

"Rose – I broke every speed limit in the country and spent three *hundred* Euro so I could catch you and beg you not to go. So I could..."

Rose bit her lower lip and held her breath.

"So I could tell you that I am madly, deeply, crazy-stupid in love with you."

Rose laughed. Because it was so absurdly wonderful she couldn't think of anything else to do.

Thomas raised his voice. "Ladies and gentlemen," he yelled. "This woman is the most incredible, kind, smart, funny, and brave person I have ever met in my life."

Rose was blushing furiously, giggling, and saying, "Shhhh, shhhh."

But Thomas continued. "And I – Thomas Goodwin – will love her for the rest of my life."

"Thomas!"

All around them, people began to clap and whoop. And, for the first time in her life, Rose didn't mind in the slightest that she was the centre of attention.

Opening up her lungs and taking a deep breath, she shouted, "I love you too!"

And then, finally, Thomas swept her up in his arms, whirled her around, and kissed her.

When he put her back down on the ground, he balanced his hat on her head and ducked beneath its rim so that he could look deep into her eyes. "So, Remarkable Rose, will you stay with me?"

"Maybe," she said, grinning. "Just, maybe."

EPILOGUE

SIX MONTHS LATER

"*A*re you looking forward to seeing her?" Thomas wrapped his arms around Rose's waist and nuzzled into her neck.

They were standing on the terrace, waiting for Katie's taxi to arrive. And Rose felt horribly nervous.

Smiling, Thomas turned Rose around and cupped her face in his hands. "It's going to be fine. We've video chatted with her hundreds of times – she's *fine* with it."

"She was fine with us dating. But will she be fine with us getting *married* Thomas?"

Thomas took Rose's left hand between both of his and kissed the top of it. "She will be over the moon. And, as soon as we've told her, so will I. Because I'll finally be able to see you wearing your engagement ring."

Rose grinned, remembering the night Thomas had proposed to her under the stars by the waterfall, when they'd danced and kissed and recreated the very first time they'd realised how they felt about each other. "It will be nice to show it off."

Thomas kissed her forehead, then the spot below her ear that always made her giggle, then just as she was about to kiss him back, he stopped and waved.

Rose turned around, already blushing furiously. In the distance, a silver taxi cab was pulling through the ranch gates.

Rose waved too and her stomach somersaulted.

It was a half-a-year since Rose had agreed to stay in Italy with Thomas. Since then, she had become the ranch's new accounts manager and had spent long glorious days helping with the horses, doing the accounts, and marvelling at the fact that she'd gone from a box cubicle in a high-rise office block to a desk that looked out at nothing but hills, horses, and blue skies.

She had not, however, seen her best friend in person. Katie's work had been incredibly busy and Thomas hadn't been able to leave the ranch either. Rose could have visited alone, but she'd been too nervous. So, they had video chatted and texted and emailed. And it had all been fine. Normal.

But now that they were about to come face-to-face, Rose felt her stomach lurch.

She wanted it to be just the way it used to be between them, and she was terrified that Katie would find it too strange to see her best friend and her brother as a couple.

Rose had asked Thomas to wait until they were sitting down for dinner before he told Katie about their engagement. But, typical Thomas, he just couldn't control his excitement.

They'd barely finished hugging and saying hello before he grabbed his sister's hands and announced, "We have some news."

Rose widened her eyes at him, praying he'd take the hint and at least let Katie get settled. But he ignored her completely.

Katie raised her eyebrows at them. "News?"

Thomas was grinning and, although Rose was annoyed that he wasn't keeping to what they'd planned, she couldn't help feeling a little flutter of pride that he was so thrilled to be marrying her.

"Yes," he said. But then he couldn't seem to get the words out. He faltered and started to blush. And eventually, Rose stepped in.

"Katie," she said, slowly. "Thomas asked me to marry him. And I said yes."

For a moment, Katie's expression didn't change. She looked from Rose to Thomas and back to Rose, utterly speechless. But then her lips spread into the most enormous grin and she let out a squeal. She waved her arms and jumped up and down and threw herself at Katie, then at Thomas, hugging them and saying, "I can't believe it! You're getting married!"

When she finally pulled away, she was crying.

"Katie?" Rose looked at her friend, utterly bemused.

Katie swiped at her cheeks. "I'm sorry," she said. "I'm just so happy to see you both and this is the most amazing news."

"It is?" Rose glanced at Thomas, who was beaming from ear-to-ear.

"Of course it is!" Katie replied. "My best friend and my brother getting married? It's the best news in the world."

Rose's heart felt so full that she couldn't contain her joy any longer. And soon she was crying too – tears of utter happiness.

"Rose!" Katie said, grinning. "We get to plan a *wedding*!"

"Uh oh." Thomas rolled his eyes. "I feel like I'm letting myself in for trouble here."

"You most definitely are," Rose replied. "Now, Mister Goodwin, where's that gorgeous ring?"

Thomas reached into his pocket then, in true Thomas-style, still wearing his ridiculous red cowboy boots and his enormous smile, he knelt down in front of her and asked her one more time:

"Rose, will you marry me?"

"Yes," she replied. "I absolutely will."

THE END

Thank you for reading **Love in Tuscany**.

Want to continue Rose and Thomas' journey? Catch up with them thirty years from now with my brand new series ***Heart of the Hills***.

Book one, ***A Heart Full of Secrets*** *is available now.*

If you love romance stories with a hint of adventure and a happy ever after, you'll also love the other books in the ***True Love Travels*** *series.*

All books are available in Kindle Unlimited, and you can grab ***Love in the Alps*** *totally free if you sign up to my mailing list.*

True Love Travels

Love in the Rockies

Love in Provence

Love in Tuscany

Love in The Highlands

Love at Christmas

Love in the Alps – Subscriber Exclusive –
poppypennington.com

THANK YOU!

Thank you so much for reading *Love in Tuscany*. It's hard for me to say just how much I appreciate my readers. Especially those who get in touch. Please always feel free to email me at poppy@poppypennington.com.

If you enjoyed this book, please consider taking a moment to leave a review on Amazon. Reviews are crucial for an author's success and I would really, sincerely appreciate it.

You can leave a review at:

amazon.com/author/poppypenningtonsmith

goodreads.com/Poppy_Pennington_Smith

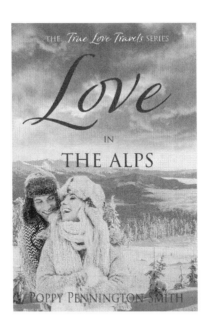

Join Poppy's mailing list to stay up to date with all of her latest releases and download the novelette *Love in the Alps* totally free!

Download Love in the Alps here:
https://BookHip.com/JCCGXV
or visit poppypennington.com

ABOUT POPPY

Poppy Pennington-Smith writes sweet, wholesome romance novels featuring tenacious women and the gorgeous guys who fall for them.

Poppy has always been a romantic at heart. A sucker for a happy ending, she loves writing books that give you a warm, fuzzy feeling.

When she's not running around after Mr. P and Mini P, Poppy can be found drinking coffee from a Frida Kahlo mug, cuddled up in a mustard yellow blanket, and watching the garden from her writing shed.

Poppy's dream-come-true is talking to readers who enjoy her books. So, please do let her know what you think of them.

You can email poppy@poppypennington.com or join the PoppyPennReaders group on Facebook to get in touch.

You can also visit www.poppypennington.com.

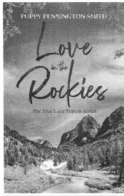

All of Poppy's
books are
free to read with
Kindle Unlimited

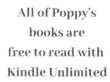

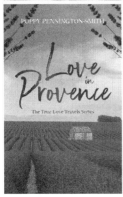

Printed in Great Britain
by Amazon